THE O꓾ LO
OF THE BAY

SEAN DIETRICH

Copyright © 2013 Sean Dietrich

ISBN-13:978-1506115511
ISBN-10:1506115519

DEDICATION

I'd like to dedicate this book to my family of natives here in Northwest Florida. It's the place that will forever live deep within the heart of me, because it is my home. We're a unique area and a unique collection of misfits, with just enough redneck in us to make our parents proud, and just enough real estate in us to make our tourists jealous.

ACKNOWLEDGMENTS

First, I'd like to acknowledge my wife for being supportive in the development of this book, and for having a sense of humor. I also want to thank my editor Amanda whose contribution, both to this book and to me personally, cannot be measured in words. I'd also like to thank the Franklin County Sheriff department for their service to the community. The selfless Franklin County Sheriff deputies serve the people of the area tirelessly.

1.

My headlights were no match for the thick Floridian fog. It was an obstinate wall of gray, suffocating the atmosphere like a wet dishrag. It's one of our trademarks. And it's deadly stuff. Fog can be a real problem where we live. People don't always realize how dangerous it really is. Throughout the year, I received more calls about fog-related accidents along our highway than I did about drinking-related accidents.

Occasionally I got calls for both.

It was as thick as soup that night. I drove at a snail's pace, watching for any sudden obstacles hidden within the miasma. My hazard lights flashing. The last thing I needed was some fool rear-ending me.

Accidents could happen in the twitch of an eyelid.

Or faster.

Through my windshield, pulled off onto the side of the road, I spotted an old yellow truck towing a fishing boat. Two silhouettes squatted down behind the boat, struggling to lift something. Through the dense fog it looked to be a dead deer. A big one. I pulled my truck onto the shoulder of the old highway, bouncing over the gravel. I left the vehicle running, swung open the door, and leapt out.

"Can I lend you boys a hand?" I called out.

I wasn't sure if I was pulling over to help them, or to admire the gigantic buck.

Startled, the boys let go of the deer. The limp thing fell to the ground like a heavy rag doll, landing contorted in the dirt. It was then that I recognized the massive frame lying on the ground.

And it was no buck.

One of the two young men bolted southward, sprinting through the dense forest toward the beach. I unholstered my sidearm and let it hang limp by my side. It was a hunting reflex. None of us in the department had any law enforcement training, unless you count shooting dove.

The other boy did not run, but stood looking at me with strong eyes. It was Gabe Alison. He laced his fingers behind his head and threw himself on the ground, face down.

Kids.

"Good God," I said. "I'm not going to shoot you, Gabe."

He was drunk.

"Get off the ground and have a seat on your tailgate, please."

The young man rose and scooted himself onto the open tailgate, squinting in the glow of my headlights. I looked down at the enormous body prone in the dirt. The barrel chest heaved upwards with each breath like a big accordion.

Still breathing, good sign.

"Gabe, was that your brother Jon Jon who just bolted toward the beach?" I asked with a little vinegar in my voice. "Because it sure as hell looked like Jon Jon."

Gabe said nothing.

"Okay, be that way," I said.

I dug my handheld radio from my coat pocket and held it close to my mouth. "You still there Hooty?"

"Still here, Jimmy," Hooty responded. "I was about to go home for the night. What's up? Over."

"I need some assistance here on the eastbound highway, about eight miles outside town. I have a subject on foot, a young man, got away from me. He's running down the beach somewhere, I think it's Jon Jon Alison."

"Copy that," the static voice cut through the fog. "I'll send Billy right over."

I looked at the huge body on the ground again.

It was a gargantuan body.

"One more thing," I said. "We got an unconscious boy here. Looks like he weighs about two fifty, maybe even two seventy-five. Tell Billy to bring a few back braces and some Tylenol."

2.

"It's called a half-duplex radio, gentlemen," the young man with the Manhattan accent said as he patted the radio receiver box. "It will either transmit or receive, but it won't do both at the same time, like a telephone does."

The man was from New York somewhere, and he didn't fit in our town, not even for a few minutes. He seemed to patronize everyone he spoke to, but it wasn't on purpose, it was just the way he talked. Everything about him, his dark features, his oiled hair, and his street jargon made him a foreigner.

My daddy picked up the radio microphone. It was silver and sleek like a miniature rocket; it looked like something from the future, or a comic book. He pressed the button and spoke into the contraption.

"Hello?" was all he could think to say.

He looked over at his deputy, Hooty, who stood wide legged, arms crossed, in a skeptical pose. Hooty who grew up in Cedar Port, who walked barefoot until he drafted into the army, whose mother cooked every meal on a wood burning stove, and whose father used a horse and wagon, wasn't enthusiastic about modernization. The most modern invention Hooty owned was a Chevy, and that was well enough.

Hooty, who was sweating through his white collared shirt, might've been more receptive to the young man if he would have acted decently, but he did not. The man from New York was abrasive, lacking the most basic manners. Everything he said seemed to squeal at a high pitch, like a wild boar. He was cocky and fast moving, wearing a broad shouldered suit, the kind that men wore in the movies, but not in real life.

The man taught Daddy and Hooty how to use the radio, but became frustrated with them, they were slow learners. By the end of the lesson, the New York yankee was on young Hooty's nerves so bad, that if they would've been in a different time and place, maybe standing around a campfire holding jars of corn liquor, Hooty would've crawled all over that yank until his new suit looked like burlap. Instead, Hooty invited the young foreigner to dinner.

"There's a radio code for every police situation you might encounter gentlemen," the man said lighting a cigar. "And you wanna use that code so no eavesdroppers can understand you on another radio nearby."

"Another radio nearby?" Daddy laughed. "I can guarantee you, this metal box right here is the only doohickey of its kind for hundreds of miles."

3.

"Why this is Brian Holbrook," Billy said. "I'd know this linebacker any-damn-where. He's a hell of a football player."

Billy stood over the gigantic body of Brian Holbrook with a flashlight, the big body laid motionless in the dirt. Billy's physique was about the same size as the Hulk prone on the ground, only older, and fatter.

"Old Brian's out cold," Billy said, nudging the body with his boot. He trained the flashlight onto the young man's face.

Calling in backup was no simple task in a small town. Our deputy, Hooty, at the office, tried to reach Billy, our only able-bodied deputy, on his home phone, but had no luck. That's because Billy wasn't at home; he was over at his cousin Joel's house watching the game. After Billy changed into more appropriate clothes, he drove his truck into the station to retrieve our one and only squad car, and even though the highways were empty at night, Billy sped through the darkness with sirens blaring and lights flashing like he was rushing to the scene of a ten car pileup.

"What were you really doing out here on the side of the road Gabe?" Billy asked, spitting dark spit onto the ground. "It's about thirty-nine degrees out here."

"We was going fishing," Gabe insisted with slurred speech. "Night fishing. When our truck broke down." Gabe gestured toward the limp body. "Brian just passed out all of a sudden; we didn't know what to do with him. We were trying to load him into the boat and take him home when you pulled up Sheriff."

Billy squatted down next to the body. "Jeezus." Billy pressed his thumb on Brian's wrist, taking his pulse. "He's breathing really slow, totally sacked out. Reckon he's gonna have a mean headache tomorrow morning."

I looked at Gabe Alison. He was a well-mannered, hard-working local boy. He and his brother Jon Jon both worked like mules to support their momma and sister; they were decent young men.

But I knew he was lying to me.

"Gabe," I said. "There's no way I can let any of you go home, not until Brian wakes up. Everyone's drunk; your truck's broke down, Jon Jon's run off, and Brian's out like a light. None of this looks very good."

Gabe sunk his head.

Billy stood with his hands on his hips, a wad of chew tucked in his cheek, watching a dark figure walk toward us.

"Looky here." Billy spit. "Here comes our little fugitive now."

4.

Captain Slogan was a kind old man, rowdy, but sweet. He was short, with a lopsided head that was shaped like a hatchet. He had faded blue eyes that looked like you could see right through them if you got up real close.

He was never sober.

At the station, Daddy kept a dock kit for the Cap, so that the Cap could shave and clean himself after spending a night in the drunk tank, which happened a lot. Somehow, in spite of all the headaches the Cap caused Daddy, Daddy liked him.

Once when I was nine, while driving home one evening, Daddy and I saw the Cap's green Ford stuck on the side of the road. The Cap was inside the little car, listening to the radio, smoking a crooked hand rolled cigarette.

"It's about time you got here," the Cap said, flicking his cigarette out the window. "I'm about to starve to death."

Daddy put his hands on his belt. "What's the problem Cap?"

"The problem? The problem is I hit a coon."

"Now Cap, a coon ain't very big. I want to know why you're pulled over on the side of the road." Daddy bent down, looking beneath the car

"I already told you, Lawrence," he said.

Older people never called Daddy by his title.

"I hit a coon that run out in front of me. And if you would have taken any longer to get here, I reckon I would've had to eat him just to

7

keep from starving." The Cap laughed and then belched.

My daddy looked back to me, sitting in the truck with a smirk on his face. Then back to the Cap. "Cap, let me drive you home, what do you say? You're way too tight to drive home tonight."

Intoxicated driving was treated different in our town back then, not like a criminal offense at all. In many small towns, driving drunk was considered a privilege, not a crime.

The Cap took off his hat, bowing his head to Daddy. "Well well, you're a county chauffeur are ya?"

My daddy walked back to the truck, opened my passenger door and looked at me. He rubbed his dry hair, closed his eyes and let out a chuckle, then a sigh. "Jimmy," he said. "You feel like driving the Sheriff's truck tonight?"

5.

The three young men were settled in the station's cell, each boy lying on a separate cot, letting the hooch work its way out of their bodies. Billy and I had to carry the heavy and unconscious Brian Holbrook into the cell and lay him on a cot. It was not easy; Holbrook was as heavy as an Alabama linebacker. They cot looked like it was going to buckle under Brian's weight.

Once back out in the parking lot, Billy leaned against the side of my truck, breathless from heavy lifting. His big belly heaved in and out with each gasp of air.

"That Brian Holbrook is heavy as a sack of hammers," he said. "He's gonna be hung over bad tomorrow."

"You sound jealous." I cranked up my truck.

"Well, I guess I am a bit jealous. Tomorrow was supposed to be my day of drinking out at the hunting camp." He spit. "Instead, I'm staying here tonight guarding the Brat Pack."

Hunting and fishing is what we did. It's almost all there was to do recreationally. Most of us grew up in a Jon Boat, with Daddy at one end, and us at the other.

"Did you see how tight-lipped those Alison boys were acting? Quiet as mice," Billy said. "I've never been that quiet when I was drunk."

"Sober them up, and then get them home," I said. "I don't know Holbrook too well, but the Alisons are good boys who had a little too much fun is all. Not an unforgivable sin."

"You're gonna let'em go? Damn, you're a softy, Jimmy."

If it had been left up to Billy, the poor Alison boys would've rotted in the state prison for running a red light.

"I prefer to call myself reasonable," I said flipping on the truck heater. "Call the wrecker first thing in the morning. I want that truck hauled in and repaired. Courtesy of the county."

"You're gonna fix their truck too?" He spat on the ground. "What then? You gonna take 'em to Disneyworld for their birthdays?"

"Lord, no." I winked. "That's almost a six-hour drive from here."

6.

Momma saved every bit of food scraps from our kitchen for Rebecca, anything worth saving she kept. A little bucket under the sink that stunk like hell held chicken innards, tendons, potato peels, leftover grits or rice, apple cores, spoiled milk, and even stink eggs.

Rebecca ate all of it, even the shells of the stink eggs. That dog would eat anything.

Momma would walk out to the porch, tap Becca's food bowl with a wood spoon, and watch old Becca emerge from the shed, like an arthritic old woman, though she was just a pup. She'd stretch her long front legs, shake off her coat, and mosey to the bowl.

A good dog will mosey more than she runs.

Becca didn't run--almost never, in fact; her fastest speed was a graceful trot. That is, unless she spotted a creature the size of a bread box or smaller out of the corner of her eye. If that happened, she'd run faster than anything you ever saw in your whole life, snapping the poor creature's neck before you could call her name.

Becca was Daddy's hound; there was no mistake about it. And Becca would've gladly replaced Momma if God had made her a human instead of a dog. She waited for Daddy to return from work every day the same way. She'd lay, depressed, on her bed in the woodshed, with a direct view of the driveway, until she saw or heard that familiar truck rolling up the drive. Then Becca's heart would ignite, her eyes glowing, looking less bloodshot than they normally were.

The only times she laid on the porch, or out in the yard, was when

Daddy was home, when all was well with the world. Otherwise, Becca lay in the woodshed, scolding herself for whatever sin she committed that drove her daddy away for so many hours.

She was a hunting hound. To my daddy, that was a dog's occupation in this world--why else would folks keep a dog? When he was hunting, he withheld his praise and admiration of her until she earned it. Whenever she'd retrieve a dead duck or squirrel, he'd look down at Becca with a warm smile, and stroke the black fur between her eyebrows gingerly. That brief moment of praise was the most wonderful thing a hound dog could ever hope to experience.

We thought that Becca only cared for Daddy, and not much for the rest of us, but we were wrong. We didn't know how much Becca loved Momma until Momma passed. Becca mourned Momma in a way that Daddy and I wished we could've. She was undignified and sad.

Sometimes, acting undignified is the rightest that can be done.

Daddy gave Becca Momma's old jacket, and I couldn't understand why. "It's what hounds do, it's how they grieve," he said, knowing something I didn't. Becca took the jacket and made a bed out of it. She breathed in Momma's smell from the jacket, and wore Momma's sorrowful fragrance, like a memory. She wouldn't leave that bed for a long while, not even to eat or drink.

7.

My morning duty was to feed the dog. Breakfast was a big event in our hound's Leah's world, we called her Lee Lee. She'd start moaning and salivating the moment she knew food was on its way. It was canned beef chili; Lee Lee thumbed her nose up at most anything else you tried to give her, everything except canned chili. She was a strange pup, but she filled that vacant spot in our lives where kids should've been. Doctor told us years ago that Delpha's insides wouldn't allow for children.

I discovered Lee Lee liked chili while on a fishing trip at Delpha's parents' cabin in Alabama. I was heating the chili up on the stove when the little pup started turning circles beside me, like Lassie does when a house is on fire. She ate the chili faster than anything we'd ever seen her eat before, and that, by God, was that.

The phone in the kitchen rang like a vibrating tambourine. The sound of it startled me. I looked at the hands on the clock above the sink. It was five fourteen in the morning.

"Hello," I said.

"Jimmy," Hooty said. "We have a situation here at the office."

"What is it, Hooty?"

"It's one of the fellas from last night. I went to check on them this morning, to see if they'd sobered up. Two of them were just fine, but big old Brian Holbrook wasn't moving at all. He was just curled up in a tight ball. I tried to wake him, but he was cold to the touch. Hell, he's dead, Jimmy."

I sighed, rubbing the back of my neck.

Hooty was all spirit with fuzzy white hair, and a lazy left eye. He'd been working at our little Sheriff's office for nearly thirty years, a deputy since Daddy had been sheriff.

"And if you don't mind me saying, Gabe and Jon Jon don't seem too upset about the whole ordeal," Hooty said. "I think I'd be a little sad if I was in a jail cell and my friend was laying there dead."

"Hooty, did you take his pulse? Are you absolutely sure he's dead?"

"One hundred percent, Jimmy. Holbrook's as dead as a trout in the boat."

Elderly people could get away with making light about death. It's their right.

8.

The game was over, and we lost. No thanks to the uncoordinated left fielder, yours truly. Us boys on the team weren't sad though, we were too young to care that much about winning or losing.

Daddy, his deputy Hooty, and the rest of us boys were all congregated around Daddy's pickup truck as the sun started to get low. Daddy was our baseball team's coach, and he celebrated the end of each game, win or lose, with a ceremonial cigarette, or three.

"How long have you and Mister Hooty been friends?" Joey asked Daddy.

Daddy said nothing, but looked over to Hooty. Daddy wasn't a very good storyteller. Hooty, on the other hand, was the best tale-spinner there ever was.

On cue, Hooty launched into a tale that drew the boys in like flies. We all listened with wide eyes and slack jaws.

"Well, it was a real pretty day, and I was out in the woods hunting squirrels. I reckon I was about thirteen-years old or so." Hooty lit a fresh cigarette, and exhaled.

"I was sitting on a stump, with my gun pointed to the sky, watching the squirrels run all over the trees like a bunch of devils when I saw this fella, not much older than me, come walking out of the clearing. He was toting a big shot gun, and was maybe fifteen-years old, the skinniest red-headed sap sucker I ever saw."

My daddy laughed, and a puff of smoke escaped his nostrils.

"He told me he was going huntin' for wild turkeys. Well, I just

15

laughed until I was blue in the face, because everyone knows we don't have no wild turkeys in our woods. But this skinny red head, Mister Lawrence here, insisted that there were lots of turkeys wandering around, said you just had to know where to find them."

Daddy smiled, watching Hooty entertain a mess of freckled boys in dusty, cheap baseball uniforms.

"So I told that skinny red head that I'd like to see him shoot this imaginary wild turkey that he claimed was out in our woods. I'd even put a little money on it."

"We walked deep back into the pines, and I mean way back where the sunshine is hard to see. Finally, we settled at a spot where we sat for several hours, just talking, waiting."

"Sure enough, out of the thicket come a big old turkey that was 'bout as big as a hog. He had the prettiest, most colorful feathers I ever seen. The skinny red headed boy held up his gun, like this, real steady, and shot. Bam!"

Hooty imitated the pose of a man holding a shotgun. And it made the story so much better.

"Well boys, you won't believe it, but he missed. So, without skipping a beat I took aim and shot the old bird down with my own gun. And it was a lucky thing I was there too, or the bird would've gotten away, and I wouldn't have no story to tell y'all. So then my new red headed friend, Mister Lawrence here, walks over to the big dead bird, picks a feather out of his tail, and puts it in his hat. Hell, seemed like a good idea, like something the Indians would do, so I done the same thing."

"Then old Lawrence pats me on the back and says, 'Well Hooty, do you believe in wild turkeys now?'"

Hooty and Daddy laughed, cigarettes dangling from their lips, sharing a type of private joke that none of us boys understood, but appreciated.

We all wanted to kill a wild turkey after that.

9.

I rode down the empty stretch of beach highway in my truck, with the heater blazing. November mornings could be brutal, forty degrees, sometimes even thirty-nine, it was enough to make any Floridian feel like the world was ending in a battle of ice and sleet. The trees along the north side of the road were orangish in the morning sunlight, the Gulf to my south was a gentle red color. The sun crept over the tree line like a golden billiard ball. I kept my eyes peeled for wild turkeys along the side of the road. It was a habit.

My radio crackled.

"You on the way in, Jimmy?" Hooty's said over the radio.

"Yep. About ten minutes away."

"Listen, I just found out from the Alison boys that Brian Holbrook had him a wife. You wanna deliver the news to her on your way in, or you want me to do it on my way home later today?"

I hated delivering bad news. It was painful to watch someone's world collapse. No one really wanted to hear what you had to say, and yet they listened with such intent. It was agonizing, the way the room seemed to expand with the sorrow, growing bigger, emptier. I remember how my Daddy's face contorted in agony when Momma died. The entire world felt like an uncomfortable place live in.

"I can do it Hooty," I said. "I'll need directions though. I don't know where Brian Holbrook lived. I didn't even know he was married."

"He lived a few houses down from where the old Ellis house was, you know, before it burned down years ago. The little brick one."

I nodded.

And that's how deputies give directions in small towns.

10.

"That's a real shiner," Momma said, dabbing my black eye with a damp dish rag.

I sat on the kitchen chair, swinging my legs above the floor; my feet didn't quite touch the ground. My left eye hurt, but not bad. Some pains were tempered by youth.

"Did you win or lose?" Momma asked, calculating the score.

Though she did not like it, she was not surprised when boys fought. In our world, fighting was a rite of passage for a boy, like riding a bike, learning to shoot, or taking a girlfriend.

Phillip Ferguson was two years older than I was. He was a vicious bully who looked for reasons to use his fists. He was someone who I tried to avoid. I had never wandered into his crosshairs before until that day.

"I don't know. I think we lost," I said.

The walloping happened while my best friend Greg and I were shore fishing on the edge of the bay. When school was out, we'd often trek to our favorite little fishing hole. It was a spot brimming with fish. Often we would drop our homemade wire pinfish traps into the water, baited with left over chicken parts, and watch our traps fill up in only a matter of minutes.

"How about your nose?" Momma wiped the dried blood from my face. "Does your nose hurt when I do this?"

That day, while Greg and I fished along the shore, we heard voices in the woods behind us, voices deeper than ours. Phillip and his toady

Carl, who were older than Greg and me, came plunging through the woods with their fishing rods in hand. They grinned when they spotted us.

Mother dabbed my face.

"It hurts bad." I closed my eyes. Momma ran her fingers along the cartilage of my swollen nose.

When they saw us, Phillip and Carl dropped their tackle, and lunged at us before we had a chance to get away. They threw us on the ground, pinned us down, and hurled their fists into our tender baby faces. I did not go down easy; I kicked and fought with every ounce of strength in my ten-year-old physique, but I was no match against Phillip Ferguson's husky frame.

We fought hard against them to no avail. Carl, who was busy walloping on Greg, let out a blood-curdling scream. Phillip, alarmed by the scream, released me and got up to investigate.

"Who did this to you?" Momma asked.

"Phillip," I told Momma.

She nodded her head.

After Phillip released me, I sprang from the ground, grabbed my fishing gear and ran deep into the woods until my legs and lungs burned. I caught up with Greg, who'd also gotten away. He leaned against a tree, trying to catch his breath. His hair was messed up, nose bloodied, clothes ripped, and he was giggling like a fool.

Greg wiped the blood from his lip, and told me that he had managed to shove a fishing hook clean through Carl's nose, sideways, right through his nostrils. Greg was delighted. It was only a minor victory, mind you, but it was better than nothing.

"Phillip Ferguson." Momma repeated the name. Her face hardened. It was a type of territorial anger that burned in her.

She rose from the table, walked to the wall phone in the kitchen, and opened her address book.

"What're you doing?" I asked, holding a red stained rag underneath my nose. But I knew what she was about to do, she was going use her words.

"I'm calling Phillip's mother," she said.

11.

I pulled up to the wood bungalow and hopped out of my truck. I walked up to the door and a pair of shabby dogs shot off the porch to greet me, running circles around me and licking my hands. The brick house was one of the cheap homes that went up in the fifties around here, back when fishing was good, and the economy was healthy.

Liza Holbrook was her married name. Her daddy was Phillip, the same who walloped me over rights to my favorite boyhood fishing hole. I'd never forgiven him for it.

Liza was an attractive young girl, with tattoos of fish, and dragons creeping up her neck. A lot of kids had tattoos in our town; it was a new drinking activity that went hand in hand with darts and billiards. Her hair was bleached, and even though she was young, her eyes weren't; it looked like she hadn't slept right in a few years.

She invited me into her house with a little hesitation. I sat on a little emerald-green-colored couch across from her. Children's toys littered the carpet in her den like a nursery. I wondered what my own den would've looked like with scattered toys. Of course, that was an outdated daydream at this stage in the game.

"You don't wear a uniform?" she asked.

"No." I looked at my jeans. "They cost too much to dry clean."

It was a tradition. The deputies in our department didn't wear uniforms, and they never had. My daddy's uniform consisted of camel-colored pants, a starched white shirt, and a wide-brimmed hat to keep the sun off his head.

"Liza, I'm not going to beat around the bush." I cleared my throat and adjusted myself on her couch. "I'm afraid that I have some bad news."

"What is it?" she asked.

"Well, it's Brian."

I put it as eloquent as I could when I told her, but I ended up using big official words that Sheriffs often use, my speech came off sounding like a heartless weather forecast.

"He was a fool," she said.

I half expected her to cry, but instead she just looked out the window.

I looked down at the carpet, knowing that my daddy would've done different in this situation. He would've delivered the news like a preacher, embraced the poor girl, let her cry on his bony shoulder, and then quoted some folksy proverb that made everyone in the room reflect on spiritual things.

My daddy never got around to teaching me how to do that.

I wished that Liza would have cried; I could've handled that. But she didn't cry. Instead the tension lingered over the room like nasty perfume.

A little child poked his head out of the hallway; his mop of messy blonde hair hung all the way down to his eyes.

"Liza, we don't know anything definite right now. I need to find out from you if Brian took any drugs or prescriptions, or if he had any health problems. Any information you have might be a help to us."

"Brian?" she laughed. "Aside from being an asshole, Brian's only health problem was that he couldn't keep it in his pants."

12.

Our town had endured exactly four killings in its history. If there had been more killings, either no one had ever heard of them, or no one ever talked about them. And if Brian Holbrook's death was indeed a murder, it would bring the total up to five.

The first alleged murder happened during the Great Depression. The Depression didn't affect our little North Floridian fishing town like it did the rest of the country. For our isolated town, times were tight, but not impossible. Problems in the far off eastern stock market couldn't make fishing any more grueling than it already was.

Doctor Adams was the town doctor in those days; he traveled by horse, not because he didn't have a car, but because he was a cheap bastard. It was a different time when being a doctor was a thankless profession. Doctors were regarded as wizards, or heretics. Some people in town loved the doctor for saving their husband from malaria; others hated him, and blamed him for their momma's death instead of blaming yellow fever.

Adams delivered a baby for the Lovelace family one July day, out in Cedar Port. Mrs. Lovelace, the mother, died during childbirth, and so did the baby. Her roughneck husband was so infuriated at the smug doctor for not saving his wife and child that he decided to strangle the poor doctor to death. Our little community, which was filled with old world fishermen, sided with Mister Lovelace on the matter.

The second and third deaths both occurred when my daddy was a newly-elected sheriff. First, it was Little Bobbie. Rumors said that he was killed over a debt of thirty dollars. It was the first time Daddy had to investigate anything, and he hated it. Asking questions, going door to door, meant flexing his authority, something that he was hesitant to do in his early days. Prying into the lives of his fellow townspeople was uncomfortable for him, and it never felt very civil.

The third death happened right in the heart of town during the middle of summer. The body of William Manning was discovered one morning, behind the hardware store, beaten to death. Daddy said it was the saddest thing he ever saw in his whole life. Even worse than the things, he saw during wartime.

Manning, who worked on a fishing boat, was a good man, the father of six children. His death meant that his children were going to live a hard knock life, barely scraping by, but as it turned out, thanks to Daddy, that did not happen.

Two of the Manning boys were on my baseball team, Aaron and Joey. They were both fine athletes. Especially compared to the talentless left fielder, me. Both of the Manning boys were tall and lean, fast, quiet, and well-mannered. Daddy picked Aaron and Joey up for baseball practice twice each week in his truck. The three of us boys would ride in the back of the pickup to and from the ball field. We became friends each baseball season and then lost touch during the school year.

On Mondays, it was always the same, after practice he drove Aaron and Joey home, and gave them two brown bags full of groceries to deliver to their momma. Courtesy of the county.

The fourth death in our town was a killing during one of our Christmas boat parades. There was no mystery about that killing, everyone saw a Stink Alison beat a poor boat captain to death on the deck of the boat, and, as a result, he went to prison for life.

Stink was Gabe and Jon Jon's daddy.

13.

The two young men, Gabe and Jon Jon, sat on their cots devouring microwaved breakfast burritos, sipping from little Styrofoam cups that were filled with Hooty's version of coffee, something that was more akin to tar.

Hooty saw me walk in, and I could tell from the devious look on his face that he'd been trying to pry information out of our boys. Hooty was masterful at manipulating unsuspecting people-- half the time they had no idea that he was even doing it.

Hooty walked toward me and his lazy eye drifted. He smiled and hitched his pants high upon his waist. He reached into the microwave, removed a breakfast sandwich for himself, and took a rather undignified bite.

"It don't add up," he said. "They're acting as tight-lipped as a couple of oysters. Nothing, not even a word."

Hooty salted his sandwich with a little white salt shaker shaped like an angel.

"Shoot Jimmy, they're good boys," Hooty said. "I don't understand it. Everyone in town knows how hard-working and honest the Alisons are. His momma and sister would die if they knew Gabe and Jon Jon were mixed up in something wicked."

Hooty looked back at the boys.

"I hope they don't have anything to do with Holbrook's misfortune and untimely death."

"Misfortune and untimely death?" I said. "What are you, Walt

Whitman?"

Billy came walking toward us with a half-eaten microwaveable breakfast burrito in his hand. His face was saggy and loose

"Lord I'm tired," Billy said. "And hungry."

"You're always hungry," Hooty said.

Billy cut his eyes at Hooty.

"You've been going all night Billy," I said. "Go home, sleep. Hooty and I can take it from here."

"Sleep?" Billy wiped his mouth with his shirtsleeve. "I'm supposed to be hunting right this very moment."

"Is that what you call hunting?" Hooty said. "I thought it was called getting drunk in a cabin."

"It is," Billy said. "But to our wives, it's called hunting."

14.

There's a special way that the daylight shines through the trees in the North Florida pine forest. The longleaf pines are like tall wooden telephone poles, with a few upper limbs here and there. There's not enough needles growing on the ragged old things to crowd out the sun, the daylight shoots through the treetops like a buckshot umbrella.

Daddy squatted down to my level and positioned the shotgun on me. Becca sat patient beside him, not even wagging her tail. He put an old dishrag between the butt of the gun and my shoulder to cushion the kick of the gun, then guided my left hand under the forestock.

There's little that's more exhilarating to an eleven-year-old boy than holding a gun in the woods.

"Keep your finger off the trigger until you're ready to fire," he whispered in a prayerful voice. Daddy loved to be outside; the lines on his face disappeared altogether whenever he was stalking something.

He stood behind me, talking as quiet as a cricket, helping me sight squirrels that were dancing in the treetops. They leapt from branch to branch, and whirled around our heads like furry birds with tails, bouncing from limb to limb.

One squirrel lingered on the side of a tree trunk in front of me; he clung to the tree in a stance that defied gravity. I thumbed the safety on the shotgun and rolled my finger around the trigger.

The blast awakened the whole forest canopy, and a hundred birds flew off their perches, evicting themselves from that part of the forest, probably for good.

"Go get 'em." Daddy patted Becca, and she leapt toward the fallen squirrel.

I'd made him so happy.

Becca came back with the squirrel held in her massive jaws, and Daddy took it by the tail, holding it up to the light.

"That was fine, Jimmy," he said, drawing out the word *fine*. "Let's keep at it. We need to shoot us about four more of these little guys. You know your momma can eat two all by herself."

15.

His feet were enormous, along with the rest of him. His giant legs were like pine logs, his torso like an oil drum, and his shoes like boats. I was stuck holding his feet.

It's quite a thing, how life is unpredictable. One morning you wake up, just like any other day, and in only a matter of hours the sheriff is carrying your dead body into a big cooler the size of a bathroom.

"Careful now, careful." Hooty guided us through the door into the morgue even though we didn't need guidance. Hooty wasn't able to help with heavy lifting at this stage of his life, but by God Hooty was able to boss.

Billy and I carried the linebacker through the door and laid him on the stainless steel table.

"He's heavier than he was last night," Billy said, breathless.

"I remember Holbrook was a hell of a ball player in his high school days," Billy said.

"That's what I heard," Hooty answered. "I'll bet he was the biggest son of a bitch out on the field. Look at his feet."

"Did he play ball the same time as Randall Evans? I can't remember," Billy asked. "Randall was the best player I ever seen."

And that's how conversations in the morgue go.

I leaned over the body and did a visual inspection of the linebacker. His firm jaw was covered in a layer of baby fat and stubble. Supporting his square shaped head was a powerful neck, also draped in a thick layer of fat.

I cut off his T-shirt with a pair of scissors.

"No, I don't think Randall and Brian played together," Hooty said.

"Randall's a couple years older than Brian was."

Underneath Holbrook's shirt was the body of a fallen star. His plump belly, solid arms, and gigantic thighs, now cold to the touch. I probed small areas of his body, feeling for anything unusual, making notes on a clipboard.

"I remember watching Brian play against Woodstock in the playoffs one year," Billy said. "Jeezus, it was like someone turned a lion loose on the field. He was unstoppable. Did you ever see him play Jimmy?"

"No. Never did," I said.

Delpha and I never went to high school football games. Childless people don't go to such events. Not because we didn't want to, mind you, but because we didn't have a dog in the hunt.

I moved to Holbrook's forearms and noticed a wound on the inside of his right forearm. I bent down closer and moved the spotlight above his forearm.

"You know," Billy said. "I wasn't too bad of a pigskin player myself back in the day, before I started eating for two." Billy clutched his big belly and shook it.

"Those days are long gone," Hooty laughed.

Billy waved him off.

"Long gone," Hooty said.

Hooty could get away with saying just about anything as long as he laughed when he said it.

Billy watched me inspect Holbrook's forearm.

"You find something, Jimmy?" Billy said.

"Yeah. I think so." I brought out the magnifying lens. "This could be something."

"What is it?" Billy asked.

He leaned in for a closer look. I could smell his tobacco breath.

"Hmm. Is that what I think it is?" I said pointing to the wound with my pen.

"Ouch," Billy said. "Looks kinda like an apple, I guess somebody tried to take a bite out of old Brian."

16.

Pickup trucks have their own smell, unlike other vehicles. I could sit in a truck blindfolded, and almost guess the make and model of it, simply by smelling the cab.

Sometimes it seems like I grew up in a truck.

It was an all-white Chevy that was dusted with North Florida red dirt. Daddy's truck was his workhorse, and it looked like one too. It was pocked, and faded, but not ugly. He used it for work, hunting, fishing, and everything else in between. Usually, the truck bed was either filled with something that needed hauling off, or loaded with something that he was hauling home.

Daddy's after-work routine was always the same. He would remove a beer from the refrigerator, pop the cap, and recline on our back porch, shirt half unbuttoned, with a newspaper and cigarette. But one day, he broke his normal routine, and did something else.

I came off our porch to see Daddy sitting in the dirt next to his truck door with a bottle in one hand, and a skinny paintbrush in the other. He worked with great care, etching a shape onto the side of his white truck door.

"Whatcha doing?" I asked.

"Painting," he mumbled, a cigarette between his lips.

Daddy was quite the artist when he wanted to be. Sometimes during church, he drew cartoons with word bubbles and passed them to me, straight-faced, when the sermon had ended. People in the pews thought he was taking sermon notes. What else would the Sheriff be doing in the middle of church? Momma would shake her head at Daddy, doodling like that, but she didn't really care that he did it. Church was only a social event; no one listened to the sermons.

"You're painting your truck? What for?" I moved to the other side of the truck and looked at the passenger side door.

"Well," he said. "I reckon visitors need to know who's riding in this truck when they visit our town. They need to know who I am."

I touched the yellow paint on the passenger door, it was still wet.

Daddy had painted perfect, symmetrical star.

17.

Gabe's truck was stinky; it smelled like old cigarettes and spilled coffee. And judging from the stains on the driver's seat, I'd say that's exactly what it was. I did some searching around in the vehicle to see what I could turn up, pretending like I knew what I was doing. Cops in a small down don't get much experience with car searches. I wore a pair of latex gloves that I'd bought from the drug store.

I looked underneath the seats, in the glove box, behind the visor, and in the ashtray. I didn't expect to find anything of value, but I was trying to be as thorough as they are on TV. In the bed of the truck was the usual, an old cooler, some tow rope, a red gas can, old Skoal tins, and a pair of jumper cables.

I heard a large vehicle coming down the road; it was the wrecking truck coming to haul the vehicle in.

I snapped off my purple latex gloves, and put them in my pocket.

Robert Lousy jumped out of the wrecking truck, and moseyed toward me. His leather boots, neon orange hat, and a camouflage shirt, were a type of rural uniform in our world.

"Hey, Sheriff," he said. Robert had known me his whole life as Jimmy, but he liked to call me Sheriff.

"Hey, wrecker," I said.

Robert was our town wrecker and mechanic, but it was more of a hobby for him, since being these weren't steady jobs where we lived. There weren't enough cars to warrant such things. His real job was raising horses. And Robert was a horseman through and through. It was something his family had done for generations.

"This Gabe Alison's truck?" he said as he squatted to look beneath the front axle of the truck

"Sure is," I said.

I tossed him the keys to the truck.

"The boys said it broke down last night."

"That's odd," he said. "I just did some work on this truck last month."

He looked at the truck with a puzzled face. He popped open the driver's side door, leapt inside, and slid the key into the ignition. The truck's engine fired up with a roar.

"Weird," he said.

Robert popped the hood and walked to the front of the car. He bent low and inspected the idling motor and reached in the engine.

"Engine's all good, just like I left it," he said.

Robert looked at me with a bewildered look on his face; he hopped back in the driver's seat of Gabe's truck, closed the door, and threw the truck into gear.

I stood on the side of the road while he drove the truck half a mile up the highway, turned it around in a lazy circle, and drove it back to where I was.

He cranked the window down and squeaked the brakes.

"Jimmy." Robert pushed the brim of his cap up. "You could take this truck to Daytona, ain't nothing wrong with this vehicle."

18.

I sat next to Momma in the kitchen in our old wood chairs, the radio playing, while both of us shucked corn. The sun was just peeking over the tree line, and Daddy was already gone for work.

I dropped the corn husks into a big metal trash can that sat in the middle of our kitchen, the can was full of the green leaves and strings of silk. Morning time was when Momma began preparing for supper. A good supper was an all-day affair for her.

Momma tossed me a hairbrush.

I scrubbed the hairbrush on the yellow corn cobs, brushing off the stringy silk that clung to the ears of corn like fur. We both scrubbed the ears of corn, in a manner that was not unlike shining shoes.

"Whatcha wanna be when you grow up, Jimmy?"

"A ball player," I said.

She nodded her head and smiled.

A baseball player was one of those characters in life that walked the line between comic books and reality. Back then, Gil Hodges and Mickey Mantle were not so different from Superman and Buck Rogers. The only difference between the two types of heroes was a ball glove and a wad of chewing tobacco.

"What position you wanna play?"

"First base."

"Hmm," she said. "Just like Gil Hodges?"

"Yep."

Baseball conversation was always good conversation.

Momma wiped her hands on her apron, brushing off the long

ribbons of corn silk that stuck to her fingers. Then she rose and set the bucket of shucked corn in the sink. She brought the flour out of the cabinet and began adding dry ingredients to a hunk of white dough on the countertop. It was Momma's biscuit batter. Momma's biscuits were revered by people in three counties. I watched her prepare the dough; it was like watching a craftsman build a chifferobe.

"Okay then, Gil Hodges," Momma said. "Go fetch your glove."

"My glove?"

"That's right, bring it here," she said.

I looked at her, furrowing my eyebrows.

"Go on now," she said. "Go fetch it."

I went out onto the porch and grabbed my glove off the nail where it hung. It hung next to my daddy's ball glove, which hung next to Momma's straw hat. I lifted the faded mitt off the hook, carried it into the kitchen, and plopped it on the table like it was a dead turkey.

Momma smiled.

She brought me a Hills Brothers can filled with bacon grease and set it on the table. She picked up the glove, dabbed a dollop of tan-colored grease onto the palm of the leather mitt and rubbed it in, turning the glove a rich mahogany color.

"See how I'm doing this?" she said.

"Yes Ma'am," I said.

"Good. Now, get to work rubbing this all over your glove."

She slid the can of grease to me.

"All first basemen know that you must keep your glove well oiled."

19.

Biscuits weren't hard to make, but good biscuits were. Loretta made good biscuits. Tall, golden, and flaky ones. They were as close to Momma's as you could get. A little different, but close enough.

Loretta set the platter of biscuits down in front of me. They were doused in a tan-colored pepper gravy. Tufts of steam curled upward from the plate.

"You ain't been here to visit me a while, Jimmy," she said. "What's the occasion?"

"I missed my breakfast this morning, and now my stomach is dog cussing me."

"Well, I'm glad for it, I don't get to see you nearly enough," she slapped my arm.

"I could tell you that I've been busy, and it'd be true."

"You ain't never too busy to eat food. Although from looking at your skinny neck, I might be wrong."

Loretta was an old woman who loved to feed me. She had been engaged to my daddy once upon a time. After Momma died. She'd never had children.

It all started right after Momma's funeral, when I was a teenager, she came over to our house almost every morning and fed Daddy and me breakfast, sometimes dinner too. We ate her food like baby hogs. We became dependent on her breakfasts. We didn't realize it until she went out of town to visit her cousins one summer, both he and I lost weight. Him more than me.

I negotiated a forkful of biscuit, gravy, and sausage, and then lapped up the whole forkful.

She watched me and smiled.

Her glowing grin reminded me of simpler times during my childhood. Mornings when she'd light the flame on our kitchen stove, and fill the house with the smell of bacon and coffee, fragrances potent enough to wake the dead, or a teenage boy. And then I remembered those thoughtless days when I was younger and less gray. All of it reminded me that I was an adult now. Too busy to eat breakfast.

Loretta pinched me. "You love biscuits more than anyone I know, Jimmy."

20.

What I love about baseball are the sounds. When a ball cracks against a wooden bat, it makes a unique noise that triggers a reaction in me. Either I want stand up and cheer, or run like hell. Another comforting sound is the dull thud of a baseball in a leather mitt; it reminded me of our front yard, of sunset. It reminded me of summer.

"Good catch," Daddy said.

The ball thumped in my glove like a stone.

I liked playing catch almost as much as I liked the sport of baseball itself – almost. It was something that my daddy and I did together in the front yard, always in the front.

Daddy had been a good ball player in his day, a natural athlete in every sense of the word. Our games of catch awakened the athlete that lived in him, if only for an hour or so.

I lobbed the ball back to him, imagining I was Gil Hodges. The ball smacked his glove, making that wonderful sound.

I never saw any pictures of my daddy from his youth, except for one solitary, black and white photograph. He was in a ball player's uniform, baggy wooly clothes, holding a baseball bat. He smiled in that innocent way that young men, who are still boys, smile. Wide-eyed, and red-cheeked.

As a young man, Daddy played ball for the Birmingham Coal Barons, an honest ball team, but it was short lived. He only played for one season before America got involved in a big world war, and Daddy was snatched up by the government. He liked to say that when he joined the army, he was given a different uniform and a different kind of bat. He was sent overseas to do what young men did in those days.

One of the lucky ones, Daddy made it back without any major wounds, except a bullet wound in the armpit. No one was quite sure how that happened. He did not talk about it.

He never played ball again after that.

It didn't matter, because I had a picture. Proof that he'd played with the Barons, proof that he was legitimate, and all my friends had seen the photograph at least a dozen times.

"Nice throw," he said.

The ball smacked in my glove.

Daddy and I looked toward the house to see Momma standing on the front porch, looking like an angel in an apron, wiping her hands with an old dish towel.

"Lawrence, honey," she said. "Hooty's on the line."

Daddy nodded, his mood shifting. He removed his glove and darted inside. After a few moments, Daddy came sweeping off the porch steps wearing a pressed shirt, like a man with business to tend to.

"Sorry to end our game, Jimmy," he said, closing his truck door.

I watched the clouds of dust kick up behind his truck as he flew down the dirt road toward town.

Momma put her hand on my shoulder.

"What happened?" I asked her.

"Oh, nothing to worry about," she smacked my bottom, rallying me indoors for supper. "Somebody's just causing a bit of trouble out in Cedar Port."

21.

Gabe and Jon Jon sat in chairs near the water cooler, watching me like chicken hawks.

"How's everyone doing today?" I asked.

"Good," the boys said in unison.

Gabe Alison, and his brother Jon Jon were from the Cedar Port community. Cedar Port was a run-down area filled with faded old wood houses, each of them with a front porch for sitting, which is what most people do on porches here. Cedar Port was situated way out in the sticks, on the other side of the bay from us. The community was filled with roughneck fishermen and mill workers who almost never caused any trouble. We received a few domestic calls now and then, but nothing serious.

"Gabe, why don't you accompany me to the parking lot? I'd like to talk with you for a minute." I said.

I smiled and motioned for Gabe to come with me.

Gabe's daddy, Stink Alison, had not been a well-loved man in our town. In fact, he'd been nothing but trouble. My daddy dealt with Stinky when he was sheriff. Stink was nothing but troublesome.

Long ago, during one of the Christmas boat parades, as the big fishing boats paraded underneath the pass, all lit in Christmas lights,

Stink got into a brawl on one of the boats. Corn liquor was no doubt involved. They lost control of the boat, and it ended up ramming into one of the huge pillars of the town's bridge. The bridge was fine, but the boat was destroyed. Stink beat the man senseless. The man had to be taken to the hospital in Pensacola, where he eventually died. Stink was sent to prison for life over the ordeal.

My daddy was glad as hell to be rid of Stink.

Gabe followed me through the front doors. He was a lean, strong boy, whose good looks betrayed his poverty. He had a gentle nature, and God knows he didn't want to be at the station any longer than he had to be, no one did.

The Alisons were a good family, one that Stink never deserved. His two boys Gabe and Jon Jon were model children, only five years apart in age, were nothing like their rambunctious daddy. They were nice-looking, hard-working, good boys. Growing up, their mother Glenda had been a stunning beauty, earning the attention of all the high school boys. And her daughter Cynthia looked just like her. Glenda was a kind, but sad woman, who labored long hours. She worked at the high school as a custodian, cleaning toilets, scrubbing blackboards, mopping halls, polishing windows, and washing dishes.

Gabe, the oldest boy, had been working since the age of nine. For almost fifteen years, Gabe had been working all over town, sweeping floors, cleaning bathrooms, and painting churches. Gabe was the kind of well-mannered, hard-working, impoverished boy that made you feel proud and sad whenever you looked at him.

The tragic Alisons were good people.

"Gabe." I patted my hand on the truck. "I need you to help me."

The boy looked down at the ground.

"Let's start with your truck," I said. "Robert came to haul it in, but there wasn't anything wrong with it, it fired right up."

Gabe didn't look up.

"This truck doesn't have any engine problems, does it?"

He did not respond.

"Gabe. What happened to Brian Holbrook last night?"

Gabe sighed. He looked at the truck with a sad face.

"It's not what it looks like, Sheriff," he said.

"Gabe, you're worrying me," I said. "I don't like to be worried."

The young man looked at me in the eyes.

"Sir, I don't want to be rude, but I'm going to be late for work."

He said it as if he were much older than twenty-seven.

22.

It was a pretty bright day the day. The round leaves on the magnolia trees shined in the sun, like giant emeralds. It was a humid summer, the kind that left you basted in your own sweat.

I rode my bike toward our house, looking at the magnolia trees instead of at the road, in a carefree manner. My baseball glove hung on one of my handlebars as I bobbed and weaved in a lazy pattern watching the dust kick up behind my tires.

From a distance, I could see Becca, our hound, lying by the side door of our house. She wasn't barking; she was whining, moaning. It struck me as odd. Becca never laid in the yard unless Daddy was home. But Daddy was still at work.

Becca bayed when she saw me, her mouth opened all the way, her voice loud enough to hear for miles.

I ditched my bike and ran up to our house as fast as I could, my thighs burning as I sprinted. I saw her, and I stopped in the yard.

Momma's hand splayed, flimsy on the concrete steps.

She lay on the stoop next to our house, twisted, a shiny halo of red encircled her head. Her eyes were open, and she wore an empty look on her face.

She fell.

That's what they said.

They said she fell.

Daddy didn't want to be the coroner that day, but there was no one else to do the job. Hooty and Daddy carried her body away, draped in our white tablecloth, now stained red; the same tablecloth Momma brought out for dinner guests. It was her table cloth. Daddy crawled in the back of the truck while Hooty drove, cradling her body in his arms, his face contorted with tears. I'd never seen either of my parents' faces look the way they did that day.

It was the last time I ever saw Momma's face.

I don't know why I didn't cry that day, but I didn't.

23.

Reverend Jason was a short, soft young preacher who'd grown up here. I remember him from when he was just a little thing, a toddler in rubber britches. The Reverend was youthful, he was patronizing, and inflexible, but at least he was trying. This was his first pastoral job, taking over our Baptist church when Brother Tom passed away.

The Reverend was no Brother Tom. No way, no how.

Brother Tom was the genuine article. He knew everyone's name in town, and their favorite flavor of ice cream, too.

"This is all going to be purple pansies." He pointed at the big flower bed, with a broad sweep of his short arms, sweating through his pressed shirt.

Cynthia and Gabe Alison stood in front of the Reverend, dressed in dirty work clothes, nodding at the Reverend's explicit instructions.

"All of these dead ferns and weeds need to be pulled out and removed by two o'clock today," he said. "That's when the professional landscapers are coming to install the pansies."

I laughed.

Perhaps, that was the difference between young Reverend Jason and myself; in my world, flowers were planted, not installed.

"Are you trying to save their souls, or put them to work?" I said, placing my hand on his soft shoulder.

"Quit micromanaging and let these two get to work," I said. "While there's still daylight left."

"Oh my," the Reverend said. "You startled me, Sheriff."

Cynthia and Gabe Alison looked at me with smirks on their faces.

Manual labor, outside in the November sun, is cleansing. The sun feels different during November, cooler maybe, not as happy as it does in the summer. Living here in the panhandle, you grow up dependent on the sunshine; you start to feel lonely if you don't feel it. Whenever the sun peeks its face through the clouds, you try to find excuses to get out and wallow in it.

The knees of my jeans were muddy as I pulled weeds alongside Gabe and Cynthia.

The Alisons were frequently hired by the church to do odd jobs, like pulling weeds, washing urinals or scrubbing baptismal tubs. I'd never worked for the church before, but since Gabe wasn't making himself available for police questioning in the traditional sense, I had to get creative.

"You don't have to help us, Sheriff," Gabe said, holding a dead fern in his hand.

"It's no big deal," I said.

I yanked on a thick stemmed weed, putting my back into it.

"I love being out in the sun," I said.

"I'm always in the sun." Gabe smiled. "I get sad when it's stuck behind the clouds."

"Me too," I said. "I'm the same way."

I looked at Gabe's brown skin, tarnished by hard labor, his dark arms slim, but thick. He was telling the truth about spending time in the sunshine. He either loved the sun, or he had convinced himself to love it.

Gabe's sister Cynthia was busy at task, tugging weeds from the soil, working on the other side of me, bone silent. She was a delicate girl, with long, brown hair and a stern face.

"Gabe," I said, stabbing at the soil with a hand shovel. "How well did you know Brian Holbrook?"

The boy's face flattened. It pained me to question him like that.

But we all have our jobs to do.

"Not very well," he said. "We weren't friends, but now and then we'd hang out."

I thrashed at the dirt with my tool, trying to remove what felt like a lopsided stone buried beneath the surface of the soil. It didn't want to budge.

"You fished together," I said.

I wrapped my fingers around the rock in the ground and pulled. It wasn't coming loose.

"Some," he said. "Not much. Mostly, I like to fish alone."

Cynthia Alison nudged me aside, without saying a word, plunging her hands into the dirt. She worked her little fingers around the rock that was buried deep in the soil with determination.

"It's no use," I said to her. "Don't bother with it. I've already tried, that rock won't budge."

Cynthia paid no attention to me, she worked digging around the rock. She pulled it loose in a matter of seconds. Then, removing the rock, she plopped it in front of me, like a cat does with a dead bird.

"Wow, nice," I said. "You're good at that."

"I'm not really," Cynthia said. "I'm just stubborn."

24.

I woke up slower than other people did. It took me at least a few hours for the blood in my body to get moving. That's why it felt wrong to be in a dressy suit before I was awake.

Daddy never wore a suit. He owned one, a tweed one, and it hung in his closet next to his army uniform, but he never wore either of them.

But today was Momma's funeral, and that demanded a suit.

I don't know why we had her funeral so early in the morning when the sun was so low. Maybe it was because Daddy had to work that day, or maybe it was because Momma started cooking early in the mornings, and Daddy wanted to honor her that way. The kitchen was vacant now. Now the kitchen felt like a graveyard.

My daddy was like a stone. He cried himself to sleep for two whole nights, baying like a dog in the other room. Then, all of a sudden, it was like someone turned off Daddy's water supply, and he was finished.

I didn't see him cry much after that.

Often, people at funerals are cold, they don't know they're being that way, they don't mean it. But they're hateful. Local people dressed in their Sunday best, walked in a mechanical line, shook hands, used common phrases that have been repeated and re-repeated so many times that they lost all meaning. It wasn't their fault, they meant well, but they did it just the same.

I remember that someone told me that my momma was leaning over the railing of heaven, watching me from up in the sky, smiling.

They might as well have hauled off and slapped me.

When the funeral was over, all the men loosened their neckties, and the women took off their earrings, and they commenced to do the most hateful thing anyone could ever do.

They went home and lived their normal happy lives.

25.

I got home from work early and did maintenance on our water heater. I tightened the waterline with my wrench while Lee Lee lay by my feet, snoring.

The hot water heater quit on Delpha the day before, and, as a result, she had sworn off bathing until I fixed the thing. The water ran cold as ice. Life without hot water, in mid-November, doesn't play out very well.

I loosened the bolts on the heater, and I thought about what a small town we lived in, how simple things were for us. In small towns, it's pretty easy to determine a cause of death, since most of the people who die are either elderly, or the victim of a car accident. But when it came to murder, we didn't have the budget, or the forensic pathologists to help us like they do on TV.

We used old-fashioned practices, archaic methods.

We asked questions.

I have vivid memories of my daddy investigating Little Bobbie's death when I was in grade school. Bobbie had been shot while he was out fishing in the bay on his little skiff. The body was found several days later. After the turkey buzzards got to it. Investigation for my daddy meant riding around town during the dinner hours, stopping at folk's houses, cordially inviting men out onto their porches, right in the middle of supper.

"You have a good chance of getting a man to talk if he's got his kids nearby." My daddy would say as he walked up to someone's porch. "Children have a way of reminding grown men of what's right and wrong."

I remember sitting in the truck, watching Daddy through the window, antlers locked with Fred Jackson in a conversation on the man's front porch. Daddy, with his hands on his belt, listening more than talking.

And so it was that Daddy unburied the truth about Little Bobbie. Fred Jackson confessed to killing Little Bobbie over a debt of thirty dollars, though Jackson never saw the inside of a prison cell--he took his own life first with a couple a gun full of birdshot.

Daddy was a poll bearer at his funeral.

My daddy hated discord. He usually sought for a middle ground between both sides, even when there was none to be had. He was an idealist, he held outdated notions that men could live in peace, and be civil to one another under the harshest of circumstances. But it just didn't work like that, not sure that it ever has, or ever will.

My wrench fell out of my hand and clanked on the cement beneath me, scaring Lee Lee from her slumber. I bent down to pick it up and cracked my forehead on a thick copper pipe that was jutting out of the back of the water heater.

I let out a moan that sounded like a barn owl.

I touched my forehead.

Blood.

26.

Loretta taught me how to make rice after Momma died. She insisted that I learned how to prepare something decent on the stove. Sure, I could quarter a deer, skin a squirrel, gut and fry a fish, and clean a toad, but none of that counted as real cooking to her. Cooking was something different altogether.

"If you're going to be a man, you need to know how to cook something else besides a hunk of fried mullet," she said pointing a spatula at me.

She pretended to have no sympathy on me, but I knew it was only an act designed to keep me from feeling sorry for myself.

On that sunny November afternoon, as I grieved the memory of my mother, Loretta Sims showed me how to make a pot of white rice. She taught me how to measure it, how much water to add to it, how to steam it, and most importantly, how to rinse it. She always rinsed her rice when it was done cooking so that it didn't stick together.

"You don't have to keep stirring the pot of rice, Jimmy. It's not going anywhere," she laughed. "You don't have to do anything but just let it cook."

After my momma had passed, Loretta became the cook for our house. She made casseroles, pot roasts, and soups that she hand-delivered to Daddy and me. But no matter how good Loretta's food was, it would never be Momma's cooking, she did everything different than Momma did. Loretta put garlic in her gravy, used a different kind of cheese in her grits, bacon grease in her creamed corn instead of butter, and she rinsed her rice. Momma never rinsed her rice.

After several years, Loretta finally convinced Daddy to propose marriage to her, but that was as far as she ever got him to go. Truthfully, I don't think he had intentions of marrying her, though she claimed different. To him, it would've been the ultimate act of unfaithfulness toward my mother.

Lorretta looked at the pot of rice steaming on the stove.

"Not bad for your first batch of rice," she said. "Congratulations, Jimmy. Now you have something that you can serve your friends besides fried mullet."

She turned on the sink faucet.

"Now that the rice is done cooking, you need to rinse it."

27.

The older I got, the more I liked the quiet mornings. Perhaps it was because my fondness for strong coffee--not Hooty's tar-baby coffee, but smooth coffee. Though it might not have been about the coffee at all, maybe it was the general quiet disposition of the sleepy world that I liked. There's something purifying about the morning hours, especially when it's still dark out.

I sat behind my desk that morning doing the true job of a county sheriff, catching up on paperwork. The office was one of the quietest places in the world at 6:30 a.m.

The phone rang, and it sounded like it was about to rattle apart into a million pieces. It was a black rotary phone that looked like it'd seen better days. I kept telling myself that we were going to get a new phone.

"Hello?"

"Hey, Jimmy. It's Francis."

Billy's wife knew we didn't have caller ID. I really needed a new phone.

"You got a second?" she asked.

"Sure, Francis. Fire away."

"Look, I'll be real quick." Her accent was as thick as Karo syrup.

"I'm having a surprise birthday party for Billy on Friday night at six-thirty, inviting a bunch of people. I wanted to invite you and Delpha. It's just a casual party, nothing fancy. I was trying to get you on the phone before Billy showed up to work."

I heard the back door open and heavy footsteps clopping through the office like a rhinoceros. Billy entered the office, and looked at me with his round face.

"Umm. Sure, Jackson," I stuttered. "That'd be great. You can count me in. Okay. Uh huh. Yes sir. Thank you."

I hung up the phone, and just stared at Billy.

I was bad at keeping secrets, and even worse at lying.

"Damn, Jimmy, what happened to your head?" Billy said, pointing at the gash on my forehead.

I sighed.

"Oh this?" I touched my wound. "I got into a fight with a water heater last night."

"Looks like the water heater won."

"Yeah, well you ought to see the water heater."

I slid my chair away from my desk and walked to the mirror in the office to inspect my forehead.

"So just yesterday afternoon," Billy said, "I saw Gabe Alison washing the church windows when I was picking Cady up from preschool. Guess what?"

I waited for Billy to go on.

"Gabe didn't even say hello to me or nothing. Pretended like he didn't even see me standing there, just kept washing the windows like I was invisible. Hand to God."

Billy raised his right hand.

"After I fed him breakfast and everything. How much you wanna bet that he's our guy?"

"It's good to see that you're not rushing into judgment," I said.

I looked at Billy and wondered how many innocent beers would die on the night of his upcoming birthday.

"Aww, come on Jimmy. You've been around long enough to know when someone's trying to hide something."

"You're right about that," I said. "There's a lot of things that make me scratch my head."

"I still can't believe you let them go home like you did," he said.

I sat down behind my desk.

"How on earth did a closed-minded backwoods hick like you become a deputy?"

"You hired me."

This man did not deserve a surprise birthday party.

"I wasn't about to keep Gabe here, with no proof of anything, knowing how his family depends on him for survival."

Billy held up his hands.

"We don't have enough information to hold anyone. We have no idea what happened to Brian Holbrook. We don't know how he died. He could've died from an appendicitis, a heart attack, a bad liver, salmonella, lost love, or fruit flies."

"Fair enough."

Billy tucked a wad of chewing tobacco in his cheek.

"By the way," he said. "The medical examiner from Mobile is coming by at eight this morning to have a look at the body. Told her we wanted a toxicology report too."

I looked at my watch.

"Well then, if you'll excuse me, I'm about to go take a breakfast break."

I stood and grabbed my coat from the rack.

"I'll go with you," Billy said. "I already had breakfast before I left, but I reckon I could always make room for another."

28.

"How many pieces of sausage you want?" he asked.

Daddy fried sausage over the little gas stove with a cigarette between his lips. The flame on the little stove licked the sides of the skillet.

"Just one piece," I said.

My eyelids were heavy as stones.

Our cabin across the bay was nothing but a shack situated on the water. It was a one-bedroom clapboard house made from pine, with a gas burning stove, a hand pump sink, and an outhouse. If it wouldn't have been so special, we would've probably realized how God-awful ugly it was, and why Momma never wanted to go there.

"How many eggs?" he asked.

"Two eggs," I said.

He tapped the spatula against the rim of the iron skillet, making it ring like a bell.

The sizzle of the sausage filled the cabin with a pleasant smell, and a wonderful crackling noise. Any noise to break the silence was a welcome friend.

Since Momma had passed, Daddy grew quiet. He had little to say to me, to anyone, and what he did say was brief. Meals were the hardest. We would face each other on opposite ends of the table, plates full of food, and listen to the sounds of our own forks scrape against Momma's china.

We ate the same things over and over again until the very idea of food had become altogether boring. Loretta's cooking had been a blessing to Daddy and me in that regard, her food was more interesting than what we cooked for ourselves. Before Loretta, we ate toast and butter for dinner.

"Toast?" he asked.

"Yes, toast please," I said.

Daddy inhaled his cigarette and rubbed it out in an old coffee mug.

Though we didn't say much to one another, there in the cabin, we were satisfied. The cabin was our refuge from the dry gray world. No one was there to ask how we were doing, how we were getting along without Momma, reminding us that we were two orphaned men. There at the cabin we were Lawrence and Jimmy, nothing more, nothing less.

Daddy was vacant, like his body was there, but he wasn't. It was as if Momma's passing was a double death, taking her body, and his soul. I watched him cook our breakfast at the counter, noticing for the first time how old he looked. Less strong. I didn't know where he was inside his head, but he wasn't there with me.

Becca lay on the floor at Daddy's feet with her head resting on her paws. Her huge cheeks were draped on the floor, and her lazy eyes half open.

"Becca," Daddy called, and her head shot up.

He threw a piece of sausage that landed right in front of Becca, and she ate it, gumming it like it was a dead rat.

He smiled at her.

Daddy was still in there somewhere.

29.

"One plate of biscuits and gravy," the young girl said sliding the plate in front of Billy.

"And one biscuit sandwich with a side of grits." She slid a plate in front of me. "Y'all enjoy."

Billy eyed the girl as she walked away and raised his eyebrows.

"Lord, Willa ain't such a little girl no more."

He shook his head.

"She's at least twenty years younger than you," I said thinking of Billy's saintly wife, Francis. "Besides, I don't think young Willa is in the market for a forty-five-year-old, beer-drinking, beardless Santa Claus."

The remark bounced off Billy like a rubber BB.

I looked at his platter. Three four-inch high biscuits were drowning in the thick tan gravy, tufts of steam curled in the air above his plate.

"I thought you said you already ate breakfast?" I said.

"I did."

He shrugged his round fat shoulders. "It's my birthday-week."

I reached for the pepper shaker, when I noticed someone standing at our table, holding a rolled up newspaper.

"Jimmy," Elmo said.

Elmo removed the cigarette from his mouth and exhaled behind him.

"Elmo," I said.

Elmo was short, slender, and narrow-shouldered. He had a face like an elf, pure silver hair, and his old skin looked like weathered wood that had been left outside too long. Elmo was the poster-boy for our town's version of a boat captain.

"I heard about Holbrook," he said.

He slid in the booth and sat next to Billy.

"You did, did you?" Billy said.

Elmo, who was forty years older than Billy, looked at the deputy and sighed.

"I'm not surprised by the news," Elmo said. "Holbrook was a spoiled little brat, only he wasn't so little."

"Elmo, did Brian work on your boat?" I asked.

"No," he said. "He worked on Shilah's boat. Shilah couldn't stand him. Holbrook was always causing some sort of trouble, always complaining. Shilah should've fired him, but hell, he was a good worker, and strong as a damn bulldozer. Could pull in a two-hundred-pound tuna all by himself."

I wiped my chin with my paper napkin and noticed that Billy was already halfway finished with his plate of food.

"The reason I come over here is to tell you what I saw the other day," he said.

Elmo dug a pack of cigarettes out of his shirt pocket.

"Do you mind?" he said.

"Go ahead," I said with a mouthful of food.

"Holbrook and Jon Jon got in a little argument on the docks." He clicked his metal lighter shut and leaned in closer. "I seen Brian shove little Jon Jon, and then I seen Jon Jon push him back with all his might. Shoved him hard enough to knock him down on his ass. Pissed off Brian so much that a few of the guys had to pull him off Jon Jon, he'd've made mincemeat out of that boy."

"When was this?" I said.

"Last week, I think," he said. "My memory ain't so good no more."

"Thing is," Elmo coughed. "Jon Jon didn't back down. He didn't look scared of Holbrook. He just looked at Brian, and yelled 'You better not touch me again or I'll kill you dead, Holbrook! Dead! You hear me?'"

"No shit?" Billy said. "Sweet little Jon Jon Alison? I would've never guessed that he was our guy. He seems so nice."

"Our guy?" I said to Billy.

"Now, now." Elmo raised his hands. "I ain't saying Jon Jon did nothing wrong. That boy is the best damn worker I ever seen, I'm not trying to get anyone in trouble. I'm just telling you what I seen."

"Thank you Elmo," I said.

I took a sip of coffee and noticed how tired Elmo looked.

"But, it's a fact, Jimmy. We all heard Jon Jon say it. I reckon that you're bound to hear about it sooner or later at the sheriff's department. I just wanted to tell you, before the story gets all screwed up on the party line. Damn gossips."

Mister Elmo was considered to be one of our town's most notorious gossips.

30.

The fuzzy, black and white images danced on Loretta's small television screen. Baseball players trotted across the field, only a few inches from my nose. Whitey Ford and Joe DiMaggio were embedded behind a thick piece of glass, playing the greatest game in the world. I sat right up next to the television, the way they warn you not to do. I'm not sure why I was holding my ball glove in my lap, but I remember that I was. It was the first time I'd watched the series on television.

I'd never watched the television before. I didn't know that I'd like it as much as I did. It's seemed like a rather dull activity, sitting still in front of a box. But I loved it. We didn't have a television, Daddy and me. He said that they were dangerous. Whatever that meant.

It wouldn't have mattered anyway; the town only picked up one station out from Dothan. Daddy and I listened to ball games on the radio, or read about them in the paper a few days later. Ball games were our shared interest, and nothing was bigger than the series. Traditionally, we listened to the World Series together with wide eyes and open ears. It was only the fourth year that they'd televised the World Series. But Daddy didn't care a thing about the World Series anymore.

I was alone in Loretta's den, watching, punching my fist into my glove. Daddy was outside, helping Loretta dig up a small dead tree stump in her yard. Occasionally, I'd peek out the window at them, on my way to the bathroom. I could see Daddy, serious, tight-lipped. I could see Loretta talking up a blue streak. I think that's why Daddy liked Loretta. She talked enough for the both of them.

Crack. The bat and ball connected.

Joltin' Joe hit a home run into the upper decks. The stadium erupted, and a little speaker on Loretta's television began to distort underneath the noise of fifty-six thousand screaming baseball fans.

Joe jogged from base to base. With confidence.

I started running around the room, like it was me running the bases.

All of a sudden, I felt ridiculous for doing that.

I looked around the empty room. There was no one to share the moment with me. Not Loretta, and certainly not Daddy. After all, it was only baseball, not real life. I turned off the television and sat in the silence, tossing my glove up in the air and catching it.

My glove smelled like bacon grease.

31.

The female medical examiner had a firm handshake, like a man's. She was an attractive young brunette, dressed in a tight-fitted pantsuit. The woman was not what Billy had expected when he'd spoken to her on the phone.

"Pleased to meet you," Billy stuttered, his cheeks looking more red than usual.

Hooty made a beeline for the woman from the back of the room, smoothing his hair, and straightening his shirt collar as he walked.

"I'm deputy Hooty," he said, like a man sixty years younger than he was. "It's a pleasure to make your acquaintance, darling."

I shook my head and ignored the mating calls of the old men.

"We're very curious as to what the toxicology report will say," I said.

"Yes, well the report will take a month to six weeks to be completed," she said. "By the way, that forehead looks nasty, you might want to get that cleaned and bandaged."

Hooty looked at me and raised his eyebrows.

The last time I had ordered a toxicology report was when Brother Tom, our ninety-year-old interim Baptist preacher, died unexpectedly. Though I'm not sure it's possible to die unexpectedly at ninety. The toxicology report said that he had overdosed from taking too many heart pills, and the examiner suggested that it was suicide. Trouble is, I knew Brother Tom; he was no suicide, anyone who knew him would know that.

After a lot of investigating, which consisted of rooting around in

Brother Tom's cabinets, I finally ruled it as an accidental death. Turned out his heart pills and his vitamin C tablets, which were identical to one another, and were both kept in the same kitchen cabinet.

Hooty led our toxicologist toward our morgue, and Billy followed close behind her with his nose to the ground.

"Billy," I called to him. "Get back here."

He turned back and looked at me.

"She doesn't need your help," I said.

Billy walked back to me like a scolded puppy.

"Jimmy, I was just going to make sure that she...."

"Yeah, I know what you were hoping for," I said. "But the county doesn't pay you to do that."

"But, it's almost my birthday."

He stomped one foot on the ground and walked out the back door.

Hooty emerged from the morgue, strutting like a teenage chicken.

"She's all set up back there to get to work."

Hooty leaned in close and whispered.

"She's going to take old Brian's tissue and fluid samples."

I waited for it.

He chuckled and raised an eyebrow.

"I wish that she'd take my samples when she's done with him."

32.

"Hand me that wrench, Jimmy," Daddy said as he lay on the floor behind the toilet.

It amazed me how he was able to work like he did, laying down, using both hands, smoking at the same time. I was in awe of how coordinated he was. I had a hard time catching a ground ball without falling on my face.

We were the only two people in the station that day as the rain hammered the world outside. The fat drops of water were the size of quarters, flooding Main Street and everyone's backyards. Momma used to call these kinds of storms redemptive rains. I never knew what that meant, but it sounded beautiful.

The toilet in the sheriff's station had sprung a leak; it was only a minor drip, but a leak nonetheless. Daddy believed that the best time to work on repair jobs was during rainy days when the rest of the world was busy being lazy.

On a day like that, trapped inside, if Daddy wouldn't have found a project to get involved in, he would've been bored stiff. He would have smoked two whole packs of cigarettes just to pass the time. The notion of Daddy ever being bored was a laughable idea; he could not stay still long enough to get bored. I never seemed to have that problem.

"Hell," he swore, careful to keep the cigarette between his lips. Swearing was part of doing fix-it jobs; it was part of working with your hands.

A high powered stream of water spewed from the back of the toilet, spraying all over the bathroom like a wild jet. The new, formed puddle behind the toilet started growing bigger.

"Dammit," Daddy said. "Go shut off the water, Jimmy. Go on now."

I ran to the utility closet and turned the red valve to shut off the water supply. The rusted valve handle snapped in my hand like a piece of brittle.

"It's busted!" I shouted.

He stood in the hallway, watching the encroaching lake grow on the bathroom floor. The water invaded that little room inch by inch, surrounding his boots.

"Lawrence," a voice called from the other room. A female voice.

"Hello, is anyone even in this damn building?"

Daddy closed his eyes, grimacing. He knew that voice.

"Get out here, Lawrence. I know you're here, I saw your truck outside. You come out here and face me."

Daddy wiped the water off of his face and hands using a rag and walked to the front of the office.

"Hello, Rena," he said.

Rena Patterson, a round, soft woman, stood there in her drenched coat. Rena Patterson was married to a logger, and in our area that meant that she was impoverished. She was standing in the little office with her legs wide, and her hands on her hips. Each member of the Patterson family possessed a grit that only poverty could buy.

"You worthless son of a bitch," I heard Rena say. "How dare you treat my husband like a common criminal? We've lived in this town since before your clan of hillbillies ever came to live here."

Rena Patterson waved her hands like a Pentecostal preacher.

"You think that because you wear that badge on your chest you're king of the town? You're nothing. You're a cracker just like we all are. You're shouldn't be arresting your own people. You're supposed to defend us."

"Rena," Daddy said. "Your husband was in the wrong, and you know it."

"My husband's never stolen a damned thing in his life!" She sounded mean as a snake.

"You don't know anything, you ignorant redneck," she said. "You're only listening to the town gossip, instead of doing your job."

My daddy took a breath, hitched his hands in his pockets, and let Rena spit her venom.

"Did you even bother to listen to my husband's side of the story, you pig-headed fool? If you would've, he would've told you that he lost his job. They gave his job to someone younger, someone cheaper. Someone who don't know nothing about cutting trees. Well you tell me, Sheriff, how's a man with no job supposed to buy groceries for his family?"

She was a woman caught in a current of anger and tears. Her eyes began to water, and she wiped them with her forearm.

"You stupid backwoods bastard, we oughta have you strung up for this. We're good people. We ain't never done nothing wrong."

Daddy leaned onto the desk and closed his eyes. Tight-lipped, listening. The calm lawman. Daddy stood there with wide open ears. I guess Rena's insults weren't really all that damaging. Not compared to crawling on a battlefield, leading a mess of nineteen-year-old boys in helmets up a hill to their deaths.

This, right here, was child's play.

"You don't know a thing about the real world," she said, throwing her hands in the sky. "I'm going to have you impeached for this."

She stomped her foot.

"You're finished Lawrence. You hear me? Finished."

Rena left, slamming the front door, rattling the walls of the office.

Daddy pinched the bridge of his nose and looked at the ground. He let out a sigh so big and heavy that he sounded like a horse. He rubbed his forehead and let the tension in the room dissipate.

Walking back toward the little bathroom, he looked at the flood that had developed while he was gone, the toilet still spraying like a fountain. The little leak had transformed the floor of the office hallway into a miniature river. If it wouldn't have been so comical, it would've been tragic.

"What's that mean?" I asked. "Impeached?"

Daddy was silent for a moment, looking at the lake on the floor.

"Oh, it's just a silly word. Don't worry about that," he said. "Mrs. Rena and her husband are good, upstanding people. They've just fallen on hard times, is all."

33.

I pulled up to the docks and watched the rain fall from the sky in big sheets. Rainy days were like in-laws. They were nice for the first few hours, but after that I was ready for them to leave. It rains a lot in the panhandle of Florida. More than many people realize.

Some folks have said that Seattle, Washington is the rainiest city in the world. They might be right for all I know. I ain't never been there, or anywhere else for that matter, so I don't know. But last month our town newspaper did a story about rainfall in the panhandle of Florida, and I learned something new. Turns out that Seattle gets thirty-five inches of rain each year, sometimes less. Whereas each year, we get seventy-one inches.

And someone had the gall to call us the Sunshine state.

I knew Jon Jon worked on the docks, doing odd jobs. It was exhausting grunt labor. He probably had hopes that the boat captains would notice him, maybe even give him a fishing job one day. Then he could finally make a decent wage. That's how good boys think.

I clomped out of my truck, boots splashing in the gray puddles. At the harbor, they used oyster shells instead of gravel to cover the parking lots. The rain was pounding on the empty parking lot. All the fishermen were snug at home that day, watching TV, enjoying their families indoors.

I could see Jon Jon down on the dock, in the rain, dressed in bright yellow foul weather gear. He was holding a long handled brush and scrubbing the sides of a fishing boat.

"Howdy," I called out, walking down the steps. "Looks like they dish the fun jobs out to you."

He was a lot skinnier than Gabe was, the younger of the two. He looked up at me and almost smiled through his yellow hood.

Almost.

The dock was slick. I walked slowly toward Jon Jon. I had horrid memories of breaking my tailbone as a fifteen-year-old on these very docks.

"Morning, Jon Jon," I said.

He walked up to me and extended his hand through the blanket of rain, like a well-mannered man twice his age. The Alison boys were the most polite boys I'd ever met. The wealthy, professionally-bred, spoiled snots in our town could've taken etiquette lessons from the Alisons.

"Morning, Sheriff," he said. "You mind if I keep scrubbing? I'm supposed to have all thirteen of these boats scrubbed today, and I want to take advantage of this rain while I got it."

"Not at all, Jon Jon. You got another brush? I'll lend you a hand."

34.

The quiet power in the Gulf of Mexico can be felt by just standing on the shore, looking at it. She just seems to go on forever and ever, like a kind of blue eternity, infinity. She's a mother of sorts, but she's indifferent to you. She can kill you and love you and the same time.

"We leave in ten minutes, boys," Hooty yelled to Daddy and me. "Get all your necessaries done."

Throwing our sacks into Captain Rodger's huge fishing boat filled me with a throbbing sense of adventure. He had lent Hooty the boat for the weekend fishing trip. Captain Rodger's was a lifelong friend of Hooty's. The three of us were preparing to go fish the open water for three days, looking for game fish, big ones. That made me excited, and excitement was rare for Daddy and me. It was hard for me to feel any enthusiasm over anything after Momma died.

Difficult for me, impossible for Daddy.

"Go on, Jimmy," Daddy shooed me. "Hurry up and go use the restroom."

The older and ganglier I got, the more Daddy barked at me. Maybe it was because I was ugly.

I ran up the dock to the restroom in afrenzy, ready to force out whatever water from my body that I could. The smooth pinewood docks were slick, faced with uneven boards. While running, I lost my footing and tumbled like a bumbling football, landing on my rump.

My frail fifteen-year old self-image was shattered.

"Jimmy!" Hooty was the first one to come running. "You alright, buddy?"

I tried to stand up, but I felt a shooting pain in my behind, beneath the thin muscle of my rump. The pain hurt with each breath I took.

Daddy and Hooty helped me to my feet. I hobbled to the fishing boat, wincing with each step. They carried me into the boat cabin and lay me on the little bunk bed.

"Think you broke your rudder," Hooty said.

"My what?" I asked.

"Your tailpiece," Daddy said, looking out the porthole window. "It's a bone in your rear. Hurts like the Dickens. You'll be fine."

We spent three days fishing the deep water, the boat floating on the face of the deep. At night, when we shined lights straight into the water, we could see gargantuan creatures swimming underneath the boat that made the hair on my arms stand up.

I fished while seated on a heap of pillows, cushioning my busted tailpiece. We fished for big game like tarpon and billfish. None of us said it out loud, but we all wanted to fight a mighty marlin on the end of our line. It was bad luck to admit such things; we all knew that.

My daddy worked on the opposite end of the massive boat than I did, and we didn't talk for the three days that we fished in the toasting sun. I understood that our vacation was for him. One where he could detach from civilization wholly, removing himself from all thought and responsibility. Those three days he smoked like a chimney and said very little to Hooty and me.

Hooty, on the other hand, was an incessant talker, he entertained me for three days with his animated stories. He fished next to me, telling tall tales, dirty jokes, and he even let me smoke a cigar. Neither of us bothered Daddy.

Sometimes, I'd see Daddy on the other end of the boat as he surveyed the vast blue Gulf, thinking, holding a rod in his hands. Out there, he didn't have to be sheriff, didn't have to act out the role of a grieving husband, or the role of a father. Out on the water, there was no Loretta to chat his head off, no one to criticize his judgments, no one to dog cuss him for doing what he thought was right, or to praise him for it either. He hated both.

I stayed out of his way for those three days.

I was getting good at doing that.

35.

"Thanks for the help, Sheriff!" Jon Jon yelled over sound of the loud rain falling on the metal roof. I could read his lips, but I couldn't hear him over the sound of the rain.

Jon Jon and I sat watching the torrent, sitting on a blood-stained wood table that was used for cleaning fish. The rain pelted the tin roof, the noise drowning out the possibility of conversation. Looking out through the huge boat-shed door, the Gulf beyond us was shrouded in a gray mist that looked thick and angry. It was beautiful in its own way.

"Don't mention it!" I yelled.

Jon Jon and I were suited in yellow rain slicks, drenched. I was out of breath from having helped him scrub the scum lines on thirteen fishing boats. The rain never let up one bit. My heart was pounding from the physical labor, reminding me that I was an old man. Young Jon Jon, on the other hand, didn't appear to have broken a sweat.

The rain subsided, and the noise faded to a dull white noise.

"Wow, what a storm!" He looked like a red-faced little boy. "I love storms."

"Well, that makes one of us," I said.

"What happened to your head, Sheriff?" He pointed to the bandage on my forehead.

"I was attacked by a hot water heater," I said.

"Looks like it was a mean one."

"Oh, yes. Ruthless."

Jon Jon sniffed his nose.

"You're here to ask me about Brian, aren't you?" He pulled off his hood and revealed those big Alison ears.

"I am." I nodded, still panting.

"Have you already talked to Gabe about it?" he asked.

"I have. But Gabe's not saying much of anything. You know that already." I removed my yellow hood. "In case you're wondering, Gabe's silence doesn't make the situation any better for either of you."

Jon Jon was quiet.

I watched him sitting there. He was fatherless, just like I was childless, we were both something-less. Him more than me.

"Jon Jon, you have a chance to help yourself, and Gabe too, if you just tell me what happened that night with Brian."

Jon Jon sighed and looked out at the Gulf.

"Sheriff, it's not at all what you think."

"Jon Jon," I said. "Did you threaten to kill Brian Holbrook?"

He brushed the water off of his nose.

"Yes. I did. I said that, but I didn't mean it," Jon Jon said. "Or maybe I did mean it. I can't even remember how I felt now. All I remember is that I was mad when I said that, I wasn't thinking straight."

"Was it because he shoved you?" I asked.

Jon Jon chuckled and then closed his eyes and exhaled. I could see his mind at work. He was imagining the terrible, nightmarish consequences of what would happen if he were convicted of murder. Horrific scenarios, amplified by youthful imagination.

"No Sheriff," he said. "Not because he shoved me."

36.

The dishes clanked in the soapy water as Loretta scrubbed them. The water looked like murky pond water, with little chunks of food floating in it.

"Your daddy and I are engaged," Loretta said handing me a wet plate to dry.

I took the plate. She looked at me with her eyebrows furrowed.

"Your daddy asked me to marry him last night," she said.

I nodded as I dried.

I knew the story hadn't happened exactly the way she was telling it, but she was hopeful. Who could blame her?

"What do you think about that, Jimmy?" she asked.

I shrugged my shoulders without saying a word. I was my father's quiet son. Sometimes nothing was the only thing I could think to say.

She sighed.

"You're gonna have to give me more than that, Jimmy. You men are too quiet to understand. It's a wonder anyone even knows your name."

I thought for a moment. I knew she didn't want to hear what lived in my heart, the agony over my mother, the awful thought of someone taking her place. Loretta wasn't interested in hearing about how my stomach ached at night when I thought about my mother's angelic face, a face that got a little harder to remember each night.

What Loretta wanted was my blessing.

"Of course, you know," she put a wet hand on my cheek, "I could never replace your mother. I wouldn't want to. But I could be your friend if you let me." Her eyes were sparkling wet, but she refused to give in to tears.

I looked at her, and tried to think of something to say, but nothing came out. My mouth was open. I wanted to give her my stamp of approval, but my voice wasn't working. I started to feel sad inside, remembering how this kitchen glowed when my momma stood in it, like the room itself were alive. Without Momma, the kitchen felt deserted, dead.

I stood there looking at Loretta with my lips quivering, not able to form a single word.

"There, there. You don't have to answer me right now. You can think about it," she bent down, embracing me. Her perfume smelled different compared to my momma's smell.

"We can talk about it later," she said.

I sniffed and realized I was crying on her shoulder.

37.

Delpha and I arrived to Billy's house thirty minutes late. We missed the part of the evening when everyone screamed happy birthday, and Billy almost pissed his pants from the shock. I was glad about missing that part.

Throughout my whole married life, Delpha and I usually arrived late. My wife had never been anywhere on time in her life, her mother had been the same way. Their tardiness had bothered me as a younger man, but not anymore; I'd adjusted to it. It was a part of living in our region. And at this stage of our lives, there was nothing so important that it couldn't wait an extra fifteen or thirty minutes. Sometimes an hour.

Billy's daughter Cady greeted us as we stood on the porch in the cool night air. Cady was about two foot high, dark red hair, wearing a pointy birthday hat, and blue frosting on her cheek.

"Hello, Cady," Delpha said in her motherly voice, one she never got to use. She leaned down to give Cady a hug before being swept away to the playroom.

It was our greatest failure as a couple, not being able to have children. It left a familiar ache in my heart. Truth is, I'm not sure that I'd've made a very good father. I was too much of a softy. Delpha, on the other hand, would've been magnificent.

I walked into the house and was greeted by Hooty, who held two beers in his hand.

"I can't seem to get a good beer buzz going in my old age," he said hobbling toward me, handing me a bottle. "Reckon I just gotta keep trying."

"Where's the birthday boy?" I asked, twisting off the cap.

"Outside, sitting on his tailgate with his younger, nicer looking buddies."

"Are we too old to fit into the group?"

"Reckon not. That is, if you're okay talking about college football," he said.

"How come no one talks about baseball anymore?" I took a pull from my beer. "I remember when baseball was the big deal."

"Not exciting enough," Hooty said. "Nobody gets carried off the field, unconscious while playing a game of baseball."

Billy and the boys were congregated around Billy's truck, all wearing thick jackets, standing beneath an outdoor flood light. Billy's truck was a fine-looking truck high off the ground. Shiny, big, and new. Billy sat on the tailgate of his truck, positioned in the center of six guys his own age. Most were smoking, chugging beer, and chewing.

These were my people. Well, to be more specific, these were my people's kids.

As Hooty and I came walking through the screen door, the boys in the group all stood up straight, and greeted us with a greeting you might give your great grandfather or your pastor.

"Evenin', Sheriff," one of them mumbled, stabbing his cigarette into the pavement. "Evenin', Mister Hooty."

"At ease, gentlemen," I said, taking a sip of my beer. "We're off the clock tonight."

A little laugh trickled through the fraternal cluster of men.

"Hey," Billy shifted his weight from one side to the other. "I was just telling them about that time when we pulled over the governor," Billy said with slurred speech. He was already good and tight, seated like Old King Cole on his tailgate.

"Oh, yeah. Great story." It was Billy's best story, his only story. The boys around the truck had heard it at least one hundred times already.

"So there we was," Billy said. "Had the radar gun out, and this car comes shootin' by doing seventy miles an hour in a thirty-five."

The speed of the car got higher each time he told the story.

"When we pulled the car over, I notice it has those silvery tinted windows. It turned out to be the damn governor of Florida. Looked just like he did in his damn television ads."

"Hell," one man said. "I thought the governor had the secret service when he traveled."

"No, not always," Billy said. "Sometimes they travel alone, just like you and me do. They have pretty normal lives."

Billy was a self-proclaimed authority on such matters.

"So I says to the governor, 'I'm gonna have to give you a ticket, boss, the law's the law.' Governor just looks at me and shakes his head, says 'How much you want?'"

"He didn't say that," one of Billy's friends said.

"He did," Billy sipped his beer. "Word for word."

Hooty and I leaned against the side of the house and watched him embellish a simple story into a pile of bull. Billy was arrogant to the core, and he would've irritated the piss outta me if he wouldn't have been so damned likable.

He was deep into his partly-factual story when Francis, his wife, came out on the stoop. She wore a sober face, holding a phone receiver with a long twisted cord trailing behind her.

Everyone looked at her.

Billy stopped his story.

"Jimmy," she said. "You might want to take this phone call."

38.

There was only one thing on earth it could be. Had to be. It was the right size, length, and weight. I let the package sit in my hands and felt the lightness of it.

I tore it open, unwrapping the six foot long, narrow gift wrapped box, littering blue paper shreds around my feet. Loretta stood watching me with a grin. Daddy sat with legs crossed, a cigarette balanced between his lips.

It was exactly what I thought it was.

"A fishing pole," Daddy said, as if seeing it for the first time.

"Not just a fishing pole, a nice fishing pole," Loretta swatted Daddy. "We had to order it special from Gayfers in Pensacola."

I knew Daddy had nothing to do with the fishing rod. She was only including Daddy because it was the right thing to do. He wouldn't have bought a fishing pole like this, not in a hundred years. It was too modern. Me, and every other boy in town, used bamboo stalks, the ones that grew behind the gas station.

I inspected the reel, and disassembled the pole, then put it back together again. It was a nice pole.

I hugged Loretta's neck.

I felt a deep gratefulness toward her. Not for the fishing rod, but for trying to warm up our house when it was so cold. For talking when Daddy wouldn't talk at all. For letting me tell her about my day, all red faced and out of breath, while Daddy sat on the back porch, empty-eyed, watching the birds in the trees. For pretending to like baseball.

My birthday came and went like a quick gust of wind, and soon my birthday was officially over, and I was one year older. A touch uglier than I'd been before. I lay in my bed late that night, and I got that aching feeling again. The one that made me feel like I wanted to run. Not just to run away, it was deeper than that. I wanted to flail, move my body, to sprint so hard across an open field that I'd tear up the soil. To exert myself so that my body would fall limp to the ground. I don't know why I wanted to do that.

I crawled out of bed. I slid on my jeans, and boots. Shoved my pocket knife in my pocket and removed a pouch of chewing tobacco hidden in my drawer. I held the fishing pole up to the moonlight shining through my window and looked at it. It was a nice pole.

The crickets didn't sing that night. I guess it was too cold for singing. I stood on the side of the bay, near to the bridge, in the dark, casting my line into the water, spitting tobacco juice on the ground. I could see my own breath in the night air, I liked that. The nicotine made my head feel light. I closed my eyes and tried to remember Momma's face while holding the fishing rod. I remembered the way she looked at Daddy when she was angry with him, the way she slept with her mouth open, and the face she made when she combed her hair.

I grieved my daddy. He didn't seem to care much for me anymore. Didn't care if I was happy or sad. He didn't care about baseball, or who won games. He didn't care about Loretta either, didn't listen to her, not really. He'd even stopped giving Becca much attention. Becca sulked around the house like an orphan. The one and only thing Daddy cared about were the people in town, the people he was obliged to care about.

We'd lost him.

The reel zipped and whined, making that wonderful high-pitched whirring sound. I cranked the reel slow, rolling in the line.

I lifted the fish out of the water, held it up in the moonlight, and it writhed like a column of glistening muscle and bone. A redfish, adorned with the typical polka dot on his tale. I unhooked him and set him back in the water. He shot away from with a splash, kicking his tail back.

I spat onto the ground and then held the pole up to the moonlight.

It was a nice pole.

39.

I drove through the dark November night, zooming down the highway, watching for deer along the sides of the road. They'd prance out into the middle of the highway and wreck a car in a heartbeat. I'd seen it time and again, especially during rutting season.

The phone call was from Stevie Dolphy. Stevie told me that he saw a young boy walking along the highway about ten miles east of our town, a desolate stretch of highway. Dolphy said that he had offered the boy a ride, but the boy refused. When Stevie got home, he called the Sheriff's office, but there was no one there. His call was forwarded from the station to Billy's house. Because that's what we do in our town. When I asked Stevie who the boy was, he said that it was Jon Jon Alison.

I left Billy's party in a hurry, leaving my wife there to hitch a ride home with Hooty and Rita. As I drove along the empty stretch of highway, the only vehicle on the road, I looked along the shoulder of the highway, hoping to see Jon Jon.

There he was in my headlights. Steadily walking eastward, looking down at his feet, freezing half to death.

I pulled over ahead of him, hopped out of the vehicle, shut the door, and left the heater blazing.

"Jon Jon!" I called out, trotting toward him. "Hey, Jon Jon!"

He stopped walking and looked at me.

"You here to arrest me?" he yelled.

"I'm just here as a friend!" I said, trudging through the grass on the side of the highway in the glow of my red taillights. I could see that Jon Jon wasn't wearing a jacket. Just a hat and several layers of T-shirts.

"You're not here to take me back?" he said.

"Nope." I could see my breath, something that doesn't happen often in Florida; it amused me when I was a kid, and still does.

"I'm not the sheriff tonight, Jon Jon," I said holding up my right hand. "Tonight, I'm just a friend."

He looked at me.

"I don't wanna go home, Sheriff. I can't go back home."

"Jon Jon, I'm not going to make you do anything you don't want to do. I promise. I told you, I'm just your friend tonight."

"You swear?" His teeth were chattering.

"Cross my heart, hope to die," I said, noticing how pale and cold he looked. "Where's your jacket? You'll freeze out here."

"Jacket?" He shook his head and let out a weak laugh. "I don't got one of those."

40.

I was sweating as I walked along the highway, carrying a little tan suitcase in my wet hand. The repetitive sounds of my feet on the grit and gravel of the road was hypnotic. I looked up at the sun; it felt as hot as it had ever been.

I'd brought all the things a fifteen-year old needed to survive. Clothes, shoes, socks, seventy-eight dollars, a hatchet, a flashlight, a small pouch of chewing tobacco, and a mess of baseball cards, for entertainment.

The hot sun felt good, shining on my hair. Burning my neck. I looked down, kicked a piece of gravel, and watched it bounce across the highway.

In a melodramatic adolescent way, I felt like the whole world hated me. I didn't feel needed. Since Momma died, Daddy and I were deficient in the most basic needs. We'd done without happiness, fun, and friendship. We didn't fight, we were too quiet to do that, but we didn't really get along either. I wasn't sure what existed between us. A kind of quiet tolerance, maybe.

I saw a shadow on the road approaching, long and black, and I heard the sound of tires rolling on the gravel behind me.

The truck pulled up next to me, wheeling at my pace. The dusty white passenger door had a yellow star painted on the side of it.

"Hey, Jimmy," he said it like a sheriff.

I didn't look at him.

"Where're you going son?" he asked.

I didn't answer.

He rolled along next to me as I walked, tires crunching on the pavement. Neither of us talking.

"I don't blame you, you know," he said. "I reckon there aren't many reasons to stick around. Feels like no one gives a damn sometimes. Hell, I think you might actually have the right idea. To just get out of here."

I looked at the side of his truck at the star painted on the side. I hated that star.

"I'm not going to try to stop you boy," he said. "I promise, I'm not. I was just coming to bring you this. You forgot it."

Daddy held my ball glove up.

I quit walking and looked at the glove. The mitt was an oiled brown color, the color of a well-maintained ball glove. I reached through the passenger window and took the glove in my hands.

"Can I say that I'm sorry, boy?" he said. He shook his head, maybe to keep from fogging up. "I don't know what I'm doing anymore. I don't know who I am."

He stopped the truck, then took his hat off and set it on the seat next to him, his sweaty hair was matted to his forehead.

"Now I know you deserve a better apology than this, Jimmy." He wiped the dust off of his dashboard. "But it's the best I can do. You know me."

I stared at my glove, listening to his rich voice, it was as slow as cold maple syrup.

"Dammit, Jimmy, I can't lose you. Not after what I've already lost. I think I'd rather die than lose someone else."

I held the glove up to my nose, smelling the scent of bacon on it.

41.

Jon Jon sat in my truck, wearing my oversized coat, with his hands in front of the heater vents. His lips were blue, and his jaw was quivering like a palmetto leaf. He would never know how close he came to freezing to death.

Oh, the blissful ignorance of youth.

I came walking out of the convenience store carrying a plastic bag and two foam cups of coffee. It was an all-night Fina gas station several miles east of our town, one that served fried chicken and tater logs. As a matter of fact, some folks in our town debated that the little service station had the best fried chicken in our entire region. If not the best chicken, period-- certainly the best tater logs you ever tasted.

I handed Jon Jon the coffee, and he held it in his hands, letting the steam warm up his nose.

"It's cold out," I said, drawing out my vowels.

"Thanks, Sheriff." He grabbed a drumstick from the greasy white paper box.

"Naaah, don't thank me," I said. "I'm glad I have an excuse to eat here. I love their fried chicken."

"Never had it." He took an enormous bite of the leg.

I watched him eat like a skinny heron.

He wiped his mouth with a paper napkin and looked out the window. "I can't go back home, Sheriff. Not ever."

He wrapped the chicken bone up in a napkin and put it in his pocket. I suppose poor people don't throw much away.

"Here, have more, Jon Jon. I can't eat it all by myself." I held the box out to him. "Get one of those tater logs. Those are the best."

"Thanks." He took a handful of food and set it on his lap. "This is really nice of you to feed me."

My eyes teared up, as I watched him silhouetted against the passenger window, wolfing down food like he hadn't eaten in a decade.

"Does anyone know you're gone, Jon Jon?" I asked.

He was silent for a moment.

"No," he said.

I nodded and said nothing more.

"But Momma'd probably want me to leave anyway."

"Why is that?"

"Because," he said. "'Cause, I'm a screw up."

"That's not true," I said. "I know for a fact that your family loves you to death."

He took another bite.

"They shouldn't, I'm not worth loving."

"That's crazy talk, Jon Jon. You're one of the most decent young men in our town. Both you and your brother. I'm not just saying that, either."

"Don't make no difference no how." He took off his hat. "We couldn't even help our own mother when she needed us."

"What are you talking about? You and your brother bust your hides to help your mother out, working like you do. Why, it's the most decent thing I've ever seen in my whole life."

"No, I don't mean that," he said, rubbing his eyes. Every paternal instinct within me surfaced, I pulled him to me, embraced him, and let him cry into my chest.

"We couldn't help her, Sheriff." He was wailing like a baying hound. "We couldn't help her."

Jon Jon gripped my jacket shoulders with tight fists. He howled into my chest with a shaky voice, clogged with snot and tears.

I pulled him tighter.

Sometimes friends don't ask questions.

42.

The chainsaw screamed like a wild boar screams when it's caught in a trap. It was a magnificent machine, cutting through the thick pine log as if it were a stick of butter.

They named it Tropical Storm George, which made it sound nicer than the ugly storm that it truly was. The storm took several pine trees down that June, leaving them scattered around our bay cabin like a bunch of matchsticks that had been dumped out of a box. Thankfully, the cabin was still intact, aside from some missing shingles.

Daddy cut the chainsaw motor off, the gas engine rumbling ceased.

The silence of the forest was deafening around us. The birds might've been singing, but we wouldn't hear them for several hours, our ears were still ringing from the noise of the chainsaw.

"You already finished moving all those heavy logs?" he said, brushing the sticky pine dust off himself.

"Yes, sir," I said, stretching my shoulders. I was a junior in high school, on the cusp of being a man, but still very much a boy.

"Well how about that. You're getting stronger, Jimmy." He nodded, out of breath, showing approval. "You'll be stronger than your old man, here, pretty soon."

I didn't get that kind of praise from him often, it was almost too much to bear.

Daddy dug a pack of cigarettes out of his shirt and removed one using his mouth. "Christ, there's a lot of work still to be done here. That storm the other night messed this place up good."

Daddy sat down on the huge pine log and looked upwards at the forest canopy. Hard work had a way of making my daddy happy. He loved to be outdoors laboring, purifying himself.

"Did I ever tell you about the first time I met your momma?"

He closed his eyes, letting the sun wash him clean.

"It was a long time ago," he said. "A long, long, long time ago. We was only eleven-years old. Babies."

Daddy lit his cigarette and clicked the lighter shut.

"She was stuck at home, with the ground itch." He laughed. "Ground itch wasn't that big of a deal to me. I got the hookworm every summer. But your momma's parents made her stay home."

Daddy's thin, white undershirt clung to him, transparent with sweat, revealing the shape of his bony shoulders. White and yellow pine chips sprinkled his oily mop of brown hair like powdered sugar.

"So there I was, out wandering behind your momma's house shooting squirrels with a slingshot that I'd made--I used to love to do that."

Daddy pretended he was shooting a slingshot with his hands.

"Your momma saw me outside with my hound, nosing around; she came out on that old porch of hers and just watched me. You know, just standing there."

I imagined what my mother's face might've looked like as a young child. Maybe like a cherub.

"Pretty girl." He breathed the smoke inside his lungs. "She was just standing there like a little bunny rabbit does."

He looked up in the sky and blew his smoke upward.

"Then the little girl just waved at me. She didn't say nothing, just waved her little hand."

I saw a droplet roll down his cheek and land on his jeans.

"I reckon she was just saying hello. You know, country people's like that. You see someone on your land, you's obliged to say hello."

I nodded.

"So," he went on. "I just raises up my hand and waves back at her like this." He lifted up his arm and waved it in the air, reliving the story.

I realized that Daddy wasn't telling his story to me at all, he was telling it to himself. He was revisiting something special. I just happened to be standing there, witnessing a moment that he kept locked away in his box of memories. It was the place inside him where that rural boy with the homemade slingshot still lived.

"I didn't know what to do," he said, wiping his eyes with his forearm. "I just wandered back home. I didn't even kill no squirrels that day. Not a one."

He pointed the cigarette at me. "That was the first time I ever laid eyes on your momma."

It was a sacred story.

43.

I watched the high school kids through my windshield; they swarmed around the school like a bunch of ants. I looked up in the sky. The sun was back in all its glory sitting in the deep blue sky. It almost looked like summer; however, it was still very cold outside.

I crawled out of my truck and stood by my headlights with a warm Styrofoam cup of coffee in my cold hands, courtesy of Loretta. Even though I was the sheriff, I felt like a nosy old man leaning against the hood of my vehicle, peering at the kids who exited the high school. Each kid walking out of the building paid notice to me and was sure to be on their best behavior.

Not exactly a bad thing.

I nodded at them.

Cynthia Alison came walking out of the building bundled up in a denim jacket and bright red mittens, clutching a book bag. She was a beautiful young girl, with long brunette hair that tossed in the wind behind her as she walked.

I waited until she was several yards away from the school steps before I approached her, so as not to draw any negative attention to her. High schoolers can be so sensitive about their image.

"Cynthia," I said, jogging to catch up with her. She did not slow down.

"Sheriff." She stopped and turned to me. Her brown eyes were stunning. "Jon Jon told me to I should expect you."

"I know, I know," I said. "I don't want to be here anymore than you do. But I have a job to do."

She didn't buy it. She just looked at me. "What happened to your forehead?" she pointed to my wound.

"Oh this? The doctor dropped me on my head when I was a baby."

She did not laugh.

"Look," I said. "Let me give you a ride home so that you don't have to walk home in this cold, and I'll promise you that I won't take any of your time. I just have a few questions. Scout's honor."

She sighed.

I noticed two bruises the size of dimes on the side of her neck. Seeing them made my blood run hot.

"Cold?" she said. "It's only forty degrees out."

"Then we can ride with the windows down?"

No laughter.

"I'm sorry, Sheriff, but you've wasted your time," she said. "I'm not going home yet. I have debate team, and then Spanish club. I'm already late."

I tipped my hat to her as she walked away.

44.

"Incoming, Jimmy!" Daddy yelled.

I looked up to see my baseball glove arcing through the air toward me. I turned through the air in circles.

I caught the ball glove.

"How about a game of catch?" he asked.

I searched his face to see if he was serious. We hadn't played catch in many years. He stood there with his glove on his hand smiling.

"Come on, it's been a while." He shifted his weight from one hip to the other and nodded at my glove.

I slid my glove over my bare left hand.

He shot the ball at me with his rocket arm. Is sped through the air in a straight white line before slapping against my leather glove.

I held the ball, and looked at it.

We threw the ball back and forth for two hours. It'd been four years since we'd done that. As the ball whizzed through the air, our world faded a little bit. The surrounding colors brightened, not much, but they brightened. He was half smiling, and so was I.

The game of catch with Daddy was different somehow. We weren't the same as we'd once been. Both of us were sadder, older. We both tried not to look at the porch, and remember the way that Momma used to stand up there in her messy apron, watching us.

"That's it, Jimmy," he said. "Good throw."

He removed his mitt and threw it at me and laughed. I took my mitt off and lobbed it at him. The mitt slapped him on the chest and we both laughed.

He walked to the refrigerator in the garage and removed two cold bottles of beer. He handed one to me with a weak grin on his face. "Here, boy."

I took the cold clear bottle in my hand.

"Only, you ain't no boy anymore." His bottle hissed as he opened it. "You're as much a man now as I am."

We sat on the porch in the setting sun, telling each other stories about Momma until our chests ached. We talked about the clothes she used to wear, the way that she loved stray cats, how she put too much pepper on her sandwiches, the way she loved to fish in the bay, what a temper she had, and how she liked to sing.

"Dammit, Jimmy." He ducked his head down. "I wish we would've had a second child, a girl."

"You mean a sister?" I asked. "Why?"

He nodded and took a pull from his beer. "I don't know. Maybe she would've looked like your mother. Maybe she'd be sitting here right now with us, with that same pretty face that your Momma had." He shrugged. "I don't know, maybe you and I would be a little less lonely."

It was the first beer I'd ever had, and it tasted like cool grief.

45.

I sat behind my desk that morning with the stack of papers in my hand, flipping pages. I looked over the medical examiner's initial report on Brian Holbrook. The report said that he was in perfect health, except for having high cholesterol--but then, everyone in our town had high cholesterol. Fried shrimp catches up with you.

I flipped the page and adjusted my reading glasses.

There had been no appendicitis, no stroke, no heart attack, no aneurysm, no head injury, no strangling or suffocation, and no signs of violence, except for the bite mark on his forearm. The next page said that the examiner had taken fluid and tissue samples from the corpse, promising a report within the next month or so.

I set the papers down and removed my glasses. Another month seemed like an eternity.

On the front of the stack of papers was a yellow post-it note with red handwriting on it. "Likely overdose" was all that was written on it.

Overdose. I ran my hands through my hair.

I heard the front door open, and voices in our lobby. I rose from my desk when I saw a woman's head peek in through my door.

"Hello? Jimmy?" she said.

"Glenda," I said. "It's been a long time. Please come in."

Tiny Glenda Alison walked into my office and I stepped forward to embrace her. She was trembling.

"How've you been?" I asked.

Glenda had been a nice looking woman during high school, not unlike her daughter, Cynthia, small and snappy. But Glenda had wasted her years of beauty on hard work and hateful men, and now she just looked small and tired.

"I'm not well," Glenda said.

"Glenda, what's wrong?" I said.

I pulled a chair out for her to sit on, positioning it on the other side of my desk. I helped her to sit down, even though she was about my age. Her shoulders and arms were solid and strong.

"I don't want to stay long, Sheriff, I'm already late for work as it is, but I had to come by here to tell you the truth. Especially after all that's been going on with my boys, and that, that...."

"Brian Holbrook," I said.

Her voice was as flimsy as a rubber band.

"Glenda," I said. "Can I get you some coffee, or water, or anything to drink?" We always had to ask that to people who came into the station, I don't know why.

"No thanks." She slid a cigarette out of her purse and waved it in the air. "Can I smoke?"

It was against the rules to smoke in the office these days.

"Absolutely, you can." I brought a lighter out of my pocket and flicked it open.

She took a long, hypnotic drag and exhaled her blue smoke into the air. It rose and accumulated around the light on the ceiling.

"It's me, Jimmy. It's all my fault."

I blinked my eyes.

"What are you talking about? What do you mean, Glenda?"

"I'm the reason for all of this, I'm the reason Brian Holbrook is dead."

46.

The terrible way that dogs mate is enough to turn your stomach. It looks violent, vicious, and downright barbaric. They growl at one another, curl their lips, and they glare their threatening, white canine teeth.

Daddy had seen it many times being raised out in the country, and he wasn't bothered by it at all. The men in his world took hound breeding very serious.

"It's just a fact of life, Jimmy," he said. "Most male hounds have an instinct to dominate. It's just the way it goes."

"What about male hounds that don't dominate?" I asked.

"Well, those're the hounds you wanna keep for hunting," he said. "Males like that make real good dogs."

That humid evening, Becca was mounted by one of the dominating male hounds from the neighbors down the street. I suppose everything was going rather typical, the way things ought to go, until the two animals started screaming in high pitched howls.

"They're stuck." Daddy slid a cigarette out of the pack.

The dogs walked in circles, attached together in their awkward painful matriculating position. It made me cringe.

Becca moaned like she was dying. She began to howl in a low voice. A kind of sound that I'd never heard her make before.

Loretta stood on the porch, half shocked, holding her hand over her mouth. We both watched the dogs struggle to detach.

The male dog was a hateful creature, angry. His teeth were exposed, growling in pain, his hips bobbing in that ugly way.

I hated him for what he was doing to Becca.

"Go get the hose, Jimmy," Daddy said with smoke drifting out of his nostrils. "A little cold water will get 'em apart."

I doused the two animals with the hose, spraying them all over, the water saturating Becca's black coat. But it did not help the situation. The animals remained glued together. Both animals just stood there looking at me while I drenched them with the hose until they were standing in a puddle of water.

I stopped spraying, and Becca just howled at me.

It was a heinous act of brutality. Becca was a battered victim while the male was getting what he wanted. Though, to be quite honest, I'm not sure what it was that the male hound actually wanted. I don't think it had anything at all to do with sex.

"It's the ugliest thing you'll ever see," Daddy said, wrinkling his nose. "But I reckon this means we're gonna have a mess of little pups running around here pretty soon."

47.

Glenda sat across from me, smoking like a freight train, one cigarette after another.

"Brian was hot after Cynthia," Glenda said, her hands shaking. "A lot of boys want her attention, but Brian was different, he just wanted her. Like she was meat."

Glenda's hair looked dry, and her face was drawn in and lined with age. She did not resemble the pretty girl she had once been in high school.

"You see, Jimmy, Brian's at least thirteen-years older than Cynthia--hell, Cynthia just turned sixteen in July."

Glenda slid another cigarette from her package.

"Seemed like every day, Brian would be sitting outside the high school, on the steps, waiting for her to pass by, so that he could make a comment about her. I hated him."

I rubbed my forehead, remembering how the boys did the same thing to Glenda when she was younger.

"One day after school, he's out there, watching her walk by, same as always. He's sitting on the steps acting like he's king of the damn world. But this time he's good and drunk."

I shifted in my seat and watched her.

"Cynthia walks past him on the sidewalk. Iit's late, after Spanish club, already dark outside. Well, he calls out at her as she goes by. He says something gross, but she just ignores him."

Glenda closed her eyes and shook her head.

"That just pissed him off," Glenda said, taking another drag from her cigarette. "So Brian gets up and grabs her arm, like he's going to have his way with her, right then and there.

"Well, when I see her fighting against Brian through the front doors of the school, I come totally unglued. I flew out the double doors, down the steps, holding a broom in my hands. I start smacking that big head of his with my broom handle as hard as I can. Whack, whack. Just like that."

Glenda wiped her nose with her shirtsleeve.

"When he finally lets her go, I yells to Cynthia, telling her to get out of here. 'Run!' I says, and she just drops her books and bolts off."

"So then Brian turns to me and says 'You little old bitch!' like he's gonna kill me."

Glenda paused and took a breath of air.

"Then he chases me around the school, I run as fast as I can from him, and finally tackles me to the ground. It was easy for him to do; I only weigh a hundred and four pounds."

Glenda began to sob, her thin eyelids closed, a straight thin line of smoke drifted from the burning cigarette between her fingers.

"I'm laying there on the ground, and I'm trying to fight against him with every ounce of strength in me, but he's got me pinned down. I can't even move against him. Then he looks at me and says, 'If I can't have Cynthia, I'm gonna have her fuckin' Momma.'

"That's when I bit him on the arm as hard as I could." Glenda held up her forearm. "Right here."

"So then he lets out a scream, and I thinks he's gonna let me go." Glenda ducked her head down. "But I wasn't that lucky, he just slaps the hell outta me, then covers my mouth."

She sat limp in her chair and dropped the cigarette from her fingers. It smoldered on the carpet. Glenda covered her face in her hands.

"He raped me, Sheriff."

48.

The mullet in the skillet of grease crackled and popped. Daddy sat at the little table, whittling at a piece of wood with his pocket knife, wholly uninterested in Loretta and I working in the kitchen.

"Careful, don't burn the fish, Jimmy," Loretta said, pointing to the skillet. Her hair was now a brighter shade of blonde than it had been a few days earlier.

I flipped the fish in the grease and watched it turn from snowy white to golden brown in the iron pan.

My momma never came to the old cabin. It wasn't a place that she liked. It was too rustic, she hated how dusty it got in between visits, how the rough wood seemed to suck up dirt and mold. She despised the primitive kitchen worst of all, and the leaky windows. Daddy loved the cabin; it was humble, but it was his. Momma wanted nothing to do with it.

"That's good, Jimmy, we can take it out of the pan now." Loretta took the fish out of the skillet and placed it onto a plate that was covered in paper napkins. "Now don't forget to check on your rice."

Loretta was a different woman than Momma was. She put on makeup, wore her hair short, and wore perfume. Her clothes were bright colored, and her shoes were new. Though, at her very core Loretta was a country girl, raised with a mess of loud brothers out in the sticks. She didn't seem to mind our ratty old cabin, not one bit.

"Did you tell Loretta who caught the mullet?" Daddy said without looking up from his whittling.

Loretta looked at me and then looked at Daddy.

Daddy shrugged.

"Well, tell me, who caught the fish?" Loretta said.

"Becca did." I pointed to Becca, who was covered in wood shavings, sleeping at Daddy's feet.

Loretta drew her face together.

"No. She did not," Loretta said.

"It's true," Daddy said. "Old girl dove right in the water and snatched it up with her mouth. Didn't even think twice about it."

Loretta crossed her arms and peered down at Becca, fast asleep. "You expect me to believe that a slow, lazy hound dog caught a mullet in her mouth? Y'all are so full of it, your eyes are turning brown."

Daddy smiled looking down at his block of wood. He liked to watch her get feisty.

"Jimmy, go check your rice." The pot of rice on the stove was bubbling.

I lifted the lid on the container.

"Don't forget to rinse it, now," she said.

49.

It was drizzling. A fine mist that fell from a dark gray sky above. The little droplets fell on the ground with gentle taps.

But it was an angry sky, boiling dark clouds up above.

My generation of men was a lot different than Daddy's generation. We didn't fight the war in Europe with nerves of steel, able to gaze steadfast into the oozing horrors of life, holding stoic faces. I was weaker than Daddy in that way, I knew that.

After hearing Glenda's account of the rape, I was a wreck. I didn't sleep at all.

Daddy pushed his screen door open.

"Hurry it up, Jimmy," Daddy said to me for the millionth time in my life. "Best time to fish the bay is either sun up or sun down, not in between."

"No one's going fishing tonight," I said, looking up at the dark sky, realizing that he was kidding.

Glenda's story was playing havoc with my emotions, stirring an empathy in me that I didn't know existed. I wanted to cry, or kill, I wasn't sure which. But it didn't much matter, I wasn't able to do either one.

I walked up to the cabin, Lee Lee prancing behind me, rain bouncing off her black and tan coat. I carried a little cooler filled with beer and sausage. Daddy was usually running low on both.

"I come bearing gifts," I said, waving a carton of Lucky Strike cigarettes in the air.

He stood in the doorway of the cabin, leaning against the door jamb door, with lily white hair, watching me walk the little path. I kept forgetting--this was his home now, no longer a weekend refuge for him.

"It's good to see you, boy." He bent at the waist to stroke Lee Lee's black and tan forehead. Dogs loved Daddy.

"What's the occasion for the visit?"

"No occasion."

He nodded and winked at me.

I kept imagining the anguish that the Alison family must've been going through, the torturous hell that no one knew anything about. Tiny Glenda, their hard-working mother, brutalized by a worthless lump of a man. I hated Brian Holbrook. I hated his name.

"I need some solitude," I said, noting how worn Daddy's face looked. His forehead and cheeks were like an old road map. "I just needed the peace and quiet for a few days."

"I can understand that." He stroked Lee Lee, she closed her eyes and opened her mouth in a doggish smile. "Well, you're at the right place. I'm good at being quiet."

Daddy rocked in his big soft, easy chair, with Lee Lee at his feet observing me as I put his groceries away in the cabinets. True to his nature, he didn't say much, just wobbled his chair back and forth, his head wreathed in a billow of cigarette smoke.

Daddy's cabinets were almost barren, just as I'd anticipated. He was the only man that I knew who could thrive on sardines, dried bread, and flat beer. It was no wonder that I was the cook of our two-man family.

There was a rapid tapping on the wood cabin door. The sound filled the room like a little machine gun. Lee Lee shot up from her resting place at Daddy's feet, and pointed her nose at the sound.

Daddy stared at the pine door, stirred, and began to rise from his chair like a crippled skeleton.

"No, Daddy, don't," I said walking toward the door, still holding a can of chili in my hand. "Let me. I'll get the door."

I clopped up to the door and swung it open.

Standing in the steady rain on the doorstep was Gabe Alison. His saggy, black T-shirt and jeans completely drenched, hanging off his lean body like a parachute. I could see his breath, little tufts of vapor in the night. He looked like he was about to freeze to death.

"Mister Hooty told me I could find you here," he said. "I just had to talk to you, Sheriff."

50.

There is no hotter place in God's creation than the roof of a house in summer. Our roof caught every atom of sunlight that fell from the sun and held it in its bosom.

The soles of my shoes were softening from walking on the white-hot roof of our little cabin. It was worse if you got down on your hands and knees, the heat was enough to take off your fingerprints.

Daddy and I were both covered in syrupy black tar that smelled strong and bitter. I was down on all fours, holding a wide gooey brush in my hand, slathering tar all over the roof of our cabin in broad strokes, filling up the cracks and crevices. Daddy worked beside me with a long handled brush, walking on the roof like a great heron.

He stood up straight for a moment.

"I don't wanna get married, Jimmy," Daddy said, swabbing the roof again. "I just don't."

I looked at him, daubing tar around the chimney. His sinewy arms locked in hard labor, a cigarette in his mouth.

"And I can't marry Loretta." He did not look up from his work. "I love her, but I don't love her like that. Wouldn't be fair to her."

A red-breasted robin landed on the rocky chimney beside Daddy. He shooed it away, swinging his hulking leather glove at it. The bird dodged Daddy's glove, hopping in the air. The bird only looked at Daddy. Daddy swatted again. The bird hurdled to the other side of the stone chimney and let out a shrill warble.

"Go on, now. You're gonna get stuck in all this tar," Daddy said to the robin, tapping his long wooden brush handle on the corner of the chimney. "Now get."

The bird leapt into the air and glided away.

"I'm only thinking of Loretta's good," Daddy said, flicking his cigarette into the air, watching it sail to the ground below us. "She deserves better. She deserves someone who loves her all the way."

I watched him there, standing against the sunlight.

He was right about that.

51.

"Momma told you?" Gabe asked. "Momma told you everything, the whole story?"

He spoke in a soft voice.

The rain was falling on the old roof of the cabin like a shower. I was satisfied that there were no leaks in the old roof, remembering how hard I worked tarring it just last month, for the one hundredth time in my life. I was always a sticky black mess afterwards after smearing pitch on the roof, had to throw away my work clothes.

The rumbling sound of thunder was oddly fitting for the conversation at hand. As if the booming had been scripted by a heavenly director.

"She told me," I nodded, seated across from Gabe.

The three of us men in the cabin had just finished a big meal of chicken that I had fried up. Our blue tin plates were scattered on the table like dead Frisbees. Oily bones with gristle still on them littered my plate. Gabe's bones had been gnawed clean. Gabe had eaten more than Daddy and me put together, and then saved his bones in a paper napkin, and tucked them in his pocket.

Gabe looked at me and then looked at the table.

"We didn't kill Brian Holbrook," Gabe said. "But I wish that we had done it. I wish we would've had the courage to do it."

Gabe was frailer than I'd ever seen him. His voice trembled, the veins in his lean neck exposed underneath the emotional strain of it all.

"See, it's not like you think. After it happened, after Brian raped Momma, Cynthia found her behind the school. Momma was all bruised up, limping," he said. "Momma told Cynthia what Brian done to her, since I guess there wasn't no earthly way she could hide it. Cynthia said she was gonna call the law." He grabbed another piece of chicken.

"But Momma stopped her. Said that she didn't want anyone in the whole world to know what happened that night, especially not the law. Not even Jon Jon and me. She was afraid of what people would think. People spreading gossip, talking bad."

The rain died down for a moment, and then started heavy again. The blankets of rainfall sounded like the irregular noise that the tide makes as it laps against the shore.

"Cynthia didn't tell us nothing, not a thing, just like Momma told her to do. Jon Jon and I didn't know hide nor hair what happened to Momma. We were a couple of ignorant saps. If we'd've known it was serious, we would've forced Cynthia to tell us. We would've made her spill it. We didn't know it was something that bad though."

He was choked up. His strong, youthful frame now hunched in his chair.

"You couldn't have known it was anything like that, Gabe." I leaned back into my chair, reigning in my spinning thoughts. My hatred for Brian Holbrook infected me.

"Don't be so hard on yourself," I said. I should have known better than to use such clichés, but it's instinctive.

He nodded.

"Momma healed up, after a month or so, her bruises went away, and I never asked another word about what happened to her."

Gabe sank lower in his chair.

"So, on that terrible night, Jon Jon and I got home from drinking out at TJ's Bar after work. We were pretty drunk, I shouldn't've been driving. We pulled into the driveway and saw Cynthia sitting in Momma's car, parked all crooked. Her hair was messed up, her clothes ripped, her makeup was all smudged on her face. She was crying. Cynthia never cries at nothing. So I knew it was bad."

"When Jon Jon and me got closer to her car, we could see someone in the passenger seat next to her, some fella who was as big as an ox. It was him, Brian."

Gabe didn't like to say that name.

I didn't like hearing it either.

"But Brian wasn't moving. Jeezus, he looked dead."

Gabe closed his eyes.

"Jon Jon and I went up to her window, and we asked Cynthia what she'd done. She told us that she killed Brian dead. Said that she'd poisoned him with sleeping pills and Gatorade."

I pinched the bridge of my nose and took in a deep breath.

"Cynthia begged us to help her get rid of Brian's body, but we were drunk, real drunk. I wasn't thinking clearly at all. Everything was happening so damn fast."

Gabe's face looked like a little boy's.

"The best idea I could come up with, being drunk as I was, was to take Brian out into the Gulf, tie several anchors around his legs, and drop him out there."

He stopped and opened his eyes.

"I mean…," he said. "I ain't a bad person."

Gabe's voice broke.

"Dammit, Sheriff." He covered his dripping eyes. "I ain't never hurt nobody in my whole life. I swear it. I don't think I have a devilish bone in my whole body."

He bored his eyes into me.

"I just didn't know what to do," he cried.

Gabe thumped his forehead on the table and buried his face in his arms, moaning openly, the wood table muffled his cries.

"I've done it, now." His voice sounded low and tired. "I'm so scared of what's going to happen to me and Jon Jon."

He sobbed, heaving his chest in and out, his breathing labored, like he was going to throw up. He looked up at me, his face was white as a sheet.

"Gabe, let's just relax," I said.

"Sheriff, I can't go to…" He was hyperventilating. "…prison, Sheriff. I can't go to…."

"Gabe?" I said, moving closer to him, sliding my arm around his shoulder. "Gabe. Calm down. Take a deep breath, son."

Gabe collapsed in the wooden chair and fell, lifeless in my arms.

52.

"Get the warm water, Jimmy," Loretta said, squatted down by Becca.

Becca's gut looked like it was going to burst open as she lay on a wool blanket, panting. The corners of her mouth were pulled up high, a kind of labored smile, her six foot tongue hanging out of her mouth.

I ran to retrieve the pot of warm water from the kitchen stove, running up the concrete steps, the same steps where Momma had fallen.

The concrete steps by the side door were the most horrific place on earth to me. It was the only bit of territory in our world that the Devil had claimed for his own. Daddy wasn't able to remove the brownish stain that had soaked into the concrete pad when Momma fell, so he painted over it with gray paint.

I returned to the shed with an enamel bowl of warm water, noticing how tired Becca looked. She lay there, weak and frail.

"Here one comes," Loretta said. "Quick. Come here, Jimmy, look."

I squatted down to see an emerging black blob ejecting from Becca's haunches. The little black puppy landed on the wool blanket, contained in a translucent sac, motionless.

"Is it dead?" I asked.

Without any hesitation, Becca used her wide tongue, licking the object until the thin membrane sac around the puppy burst like a soap bubble.

The puppy looked like a wet, blind, black hamster that had been wadded up into a ball. Becca cleaned the pup, washing every bit of birth fluid off it with her tongue. Then she collapsed in pleasant exhaustion.

"No, she's not dead," Loretta said, engrossed in her midwifery.

"She's beautiful. Let's call her Leah."

The pup started to crawl on its belly, in a wobbling motion. It wandered around the wool blanket blind, like a little slug.

"That's a good girl, Lee Lee," Loretta said to the pup.

My heart was light as a feather, watching the pup crawl, I don't know why. Maybe it was in my people's blood, to love dogs the way we did.

I reached out to stroke the little thing.

"No, no." Loretta grabbed my hand. "Don't touch her. Don't touch Lee Lee, or any of the other puppies. Becca won't have anything to do with them if you get your human scent on them."

I pulled my hand back.

More puppies followed in the same way, eight more, one after another, until Becca was wasted. She laid on her side, almost unconscious, except for her labored panting.

Loretta grinned at Becca.

"She's going to be tired for a while," Loretta said as the puppies congregated around their mother's warm belly.

"Is Becca okay?" I asked.

"Oh, she's perfect," Loretta said in her thick accent. "This is what God made women to do, Jimmy; it's our purpose. Take a good look at her. This is the happiest Becca will ever be."

I watched Lee Lee waddle around the wool blanket like a fat worm, searching for her mother, her eyes like little slits glued shut.

In that moment, I felt a muscle cramp underneath my ears, in my jaw, and my cheeks were sore.

I realized that I'd been smiling through the whole ordeal.

53.

"Rise and shine, Gabe," I said standing over his bunk. I'd always wanted to say that, but I'd never had any kids to say it to.

"The best time to fish the bay is either sun up, or sundown, not in between." Another family phrase that I'd always wanted to say.

Gabe stirred in his bunk bed like a boy rising from his grave. I looked at him lying there, strong and lean; suddenly I felt like an old man.

He sat up in his bunk, groggy. It was a rough night.

"Coffee's on the stove," I said walking away.

"Thanks," he said.

The bay was dark and smooth, like a piece of paned glass. The bay is a redeeming place to be. I've always felt that there are a few spots in our bay that resemble heaven. But I'm sure I'm wrong. Heaven can't be as graceful as our bay is. Out on the bay, there's a whole lot of water between a man and his problems, an entire continent of water. The water is impartial, too; it doesn't have any opinions about anything.

The sun wasn't up yet, but the birds were everywhere, and that meant fishing was going to be good that morning. Maybe even great.

The three of us, and one hound, glided across the water seated in the boat. It was an old beat up wooden skiff that was about as old as I was. Gabe sat at the bow of the boat as we zoomed forward, his eyes closed, the wind blowing his hair backwards. Daddy sat behind him, holding on to Lee Lee while I manned the outboard motor in the rear of the boat.

We trolled along in the early darkness of the morning, fishing for whatever would bite. None of us talked, but sat quiet in the boat, clutching our poles. Our wooden boat drifted in the gentle meandering movements of the water.

It was clear after a few minutes of fishing that Gabe was the most skilled fisherman out of us all. Though, all three of us were skilled at being quiet. We caught five redfish, three mullet, and one speckled trout altogether. Filled up our cooler.

In my book, that's a good day.

"Sheriff?" Gabe broke the silence, holding the fishing rod in his hands. "You're not going to arrest me?"

Daddy looked at me.

Daddy and I were never quite sure which one of us was Sheriff when we were together in the same place, at the same time. One of us bore the title, the other one wrote the book.

"Gabe," Daddy said. "Jimmy ain't wearing no badge on his chest right now," Daddy nodded toward me. "Out here, there ain't no sheriff. We're your friends, plain and simple. And right now, we's just fishing."

Gabe furrowed his eyebrows, thought for a moment and looked outwards at the tree line in the distance. The sun was a tiny slice of red peeking over the pines.

"My God, that's pretty," Daddy pointed.

Just then, a pelican swooped down in front of our boat, dive-bombing a fish. He crashed into the water with a big splash, scaring away every trout in that part of the bay. The bird emerged from the water holding a small redfish in his jaws that flopped, the fish clinging to life. The pelican looked at us with unblinking eyes, holding the fish firm in his mouth. He tossed the redfish up into the air and then caught it like a circus seal, swallowing the fish whole.

"Would you look at that?" Daddy shook his head. "He stole my damn fish."

Gabe and I laughed.

"Well, he was probably hungrier than I was," Daddy said.

Gabe stared at the pelican as he flew away, probably wishing that he could spread his wings and fly away too. If only Gabe would've known how many times that I'd wished the very same thing, maybe then he wouldn't have felt so alone.

"Why are you doing this?" Gabe asked. "I'm a criminal, I know that we're all going to jail for what we done, but instead I'm out here fishing, like everything's okay."

Neither of us answered him.

We were both off the clock.

The three of us watched the sun ascend above the horizon. It was reddish orange, like a globe of fire wandering toward heaven. I never got tired of seeing it. The morning started to get brighter, releasing a symphony of animal noises that traveled across the face of the water. The world was waking up.

Daddy slapped his thighs with his hands.

"Okay, let's call it quits." Daddy winked, firing up the outboard boat motor. "Let's go eat breakfast."

When the boat was in motion, Lee Lee stood at the bow of the boat next to Gabe, like she was leading the way. Her face was pointed to the wind, and her ears flew backward. Gabe patted her rib cage with his hand. I smiled watching them. Lee Lee was one of the few creatures on the planet who knew how to cure depression.

We trolled along the shoreline, inching toward home, the water was as slick as a varnished table top. I remembered how Momma used to polish all of our furniture with mayonnaise, like all the country people in her family did. It was a strange memory to have.

Nearing the cabin, we saw a figure standing near the water's edge.

Lee Lee barked, jerking her head.

It was a strange sight to see someone standing on the shore outside the cabin. We didn't have any neighbors, in fact, not many people even knew the little cabin was even there. The figure stood on the shore waving both of his arms in the air, back and forth.

He was trying to flag us down.

Daddy squinted at the shoreline. "What in the world?" he said.

Lee Lee whined and moaned.

"Oh my God!" Gabe said. "It's Jon Jon."

54.

"You know, I don't think you have ever loved me," Loretta shouted at my father. "Not really. And I know why. It's because I'm not her, your saintly wife."

Loretta ducked her head. "God rest her soul."

Then she stabbed her finger into Daddy's chest.

"You wanna hear something awful? Sometimes I wish I weren't me." Loretta's voice broke. "Sometimes I wish I were her instead. But I can't change myself, not for you, not for anyone, and I shouldn't have to."

Daddy stood against the refrigerator, arms folded, head down.

"If you can't love me, the very least you can do is treat me with some common respect. Treat me decent. Marry me, I mean. You owe it to me," she said. "I'm tired of people referring to me as Lawrence's friend, I'm a lot more than your friend, and we both know it."

Momma used to say that Daddy was a hard man to fight with, he was too quiet. The more you carried on, the quieter he'd get. I guess Loretta hadn't learned that yet.

"I just…," Daddy replied and then stopped. I guess he wasn't able to come up with anything better to say than that.

She looked and shook her head.

"You just what?" she asked. "You don't know what to say? How about thanking me? How about showing some gratitude to me? I've been right here in this kitchen, almost every day for four years since your wife died? How about saying thank you?"

Loretta removed her apron and tossed it at my daddy.

"I've given myself to you," she said. "It was because I thought you loved me, Lawrence. I thought you loved me like I love you. But you tricked me. You don't care a thing about me."

"Now that's not exactly true," Daddy said.

Daddy didn't look up at her.

"I thought we were going to be married. That's what you told me."

"Loretta." He sighed, shaking his head, still looking at the wadded up apron on the floor. "I never said those words exactly."

"No?" she scoffed. "Okay. So I'm a liar, is that it? This has all been one big fantasy, none of it's been real."

Loretta stormed out of the kitchen.

She walked back to Daddy's bedroom and began to pack the few things she kept at our house. She tossed her clothes into a bag, along with the other trinkets she kept in Daddy's bathroom. It terrified me to think that she was leaving us; she was the light of our household.

She clomped back into the kitchen with her bag in hand.

"Lawrence, I'm leaving," she said. "For good."

She waited for a response from him, but there was none.

Daddy tightened his mouth together.

"Okay then," she said, bearing the full weight of the one-sided conversation.

Loretta walked out of the kitchen, not looking behind her, and let the screen door slap shut.

Daddy never moved from his position, leaning against the refrigerator. He lifted a cigarette to his lips and clicked open his lighter.

"Go to bed, Jimmy," he said. "It's late."

I stood there looking at him.

"Go on, now, dammit," he said.

55.

"I'm going with you, dammit," Daddy said, sliding on his flannel jacket. He had a way of proclaiming things, like they were written in the county law book. "Quit telling me what to do," he said. "I ain't your boy."

Daddy and I crawled into my blue truck and cranked the engine. I flipped on the heater for Daddy.

"God Almighty, it's cold." I rubbed my hands together.

Jon Jon had showed us the suicide note left by Cynthia. The note was written on floral paper, in curly handwriting. She wrote that she was going to end it all on the beach somewhere.

Trouble was, we had thirty miles of beach.

"You boys drive east on the highway," I shouted out the window. "We'll drive west. We can cover more ground that way."

Gabe and Jon Jon leapt into their old yellow truck, and sped out of the driveway in a flash, kicking up a rooster tail of gravel behind them. Their engine motor screamed through the tall forest like an airplane flying too close to the ground.

Daddy and I sped down the empty highway, the sun glaring through the windshield, driving westward along the beach road. We squinted at every car we saw, studying. The beaches were empty that cold November day; no one in their right mind would've been down there in such chilly weather.

"What's the make of car we're looking for again?" Daddy asked.

"Burgundy Ford Escort," I answered, scanning the sides of the road. "An older model."

"Old to you, and old to me are two different things," he said.

"There!" I said.

I slammed on the brakes, screeching my tires on the road.

My truck fishtailed on the highway, Daddy held on to the handle above his seat to keep from flying out of the windshield. My tires squealed on the pavement and I checked my mirror to make sure we weren't about to be rear-ended.

I muscled the wheel of the truck, arcing into the sandy public beach access parking lot.

The vacant burgundy car sat there, parked crooked between the lines, the driver's door swung wide open. The cockpit light still on.

"Oh my God," I said. "I see her."

56.

"Jimmy, you're up. We're missing a catcher," he said, with a little stubby cigar tucked in the corner of his mouth. "Goodin is absent; we don't have anyone else for this game, so you'll have to do. Go on now, get suited."

It wasn't the highest compliment I'd ever received, but our hardened high school baseball coach had never understood why I even attempted to play the game in the first place. Being that I didn't have the talent for it.

Our pitcher, Ricky, helped me suit up. The setting sun blazed through the dugout windows, making a pattern on the cinderblock walls. Together we assembled the puzzle of catcher's equipment that hung on my lanky body. He draped the red chest protector over the front of my uniform, tightening the waistband as tight as he could.

"It's loose around my waist," I said.

"That's as tight as it goes, it'll have to do," he cinched the belt with a tug.

Ricky squatted down, and secured the shin guards to my skinny legs, and gave me a fat, leather mitt to replace my usual ball glove. I placed the mask over my face and looked at the world from behind the protective wire grid-work.

"Here, you're gonna want to wear this." He held up a cup-shaped object in his hand. "It goes over your, well, you know."

I sensed that it was an important piece of equipment.

"So where's Goodin?" I asked. "Why isn't he here?"

"Sick," Ricky said, tightening the strap to my face mask. "Goodin came down with the throw up virus. Had to leave school early today."

"Why me?" I asked. "Why not ask Sweet Face, or Charles to be catcher?"

Ricky shrugged.

"Sweet Face isn't here, and Charles is playing second." Ricky slapped my back. "It's you, big man."

The clear summer air was perfect for playing a ball. The humid fragrant smells of the pines were always stronger during a ball game. I don't know why. The merry chirps of the katydids and crickets blaring out of the woods behind the baseball field, sounded like a summer choir.

When the game was through, our team merged onto the field in a type of standing dog pile, smacking each other on the bottoms, butting heads, screaming, punching one another, half embracing, and lots of jumping.

"Good game, Jimmy!" Ricky said, taking me into a headlock, scrubbing his knuckles on my ball cap. "You sure showed them, you did great!"

Behind Ricky, standing there on the field, was a girl. She was a medium build, with brunette hair pulled back into a thick ponytail, showing her big ears. She stood with her hands clasped behind her.

"Are you Jimmy?" she asked me.

I pushed Ricky away with every bit of strength I possessed. He tumbled backwards, rolling on the dirt near the pitcher's mound.

He sat there laughing.

"You're a quiet one, aren't you?" she said.

She brushed the red dust off my uniform and straightened the collar of my shirt without invitation.

"Uh, yes, I'm Jimmy." I removed my hat, smoothing my hair.

"Oh yeah, I almost forgot," Ricky said, standing up from the ground, his uniform now covered in dust. "This is Delpha. She's Goodin's girl. She needs a catcher to take her to the after-game party tonight."

She smiled.

"You ain't got to wear any special gear for this kind of game." Ricky nodded to Delpha. "Though, Delpha is pretty feisty."

57.

Cynthia bobbed like a popping cork in the Gulf. She floated in the icy cold olive-green water a hundred yards from the shore like a log of driftwood. She would be dead in a matter of a few minutes.

Maybe less.

I ran toward the expansive dark water as fast as my legs could carry me. My lungs inhaling the icy humid air. I ran to the water's edge, my legs were numb from the cold.

I kicked off my boots and discarded my jacket.

Plunging into the water was a shock to my system; it was as cold as an ice bath. I swam out to Cynthia as fast as my rickety body would move, reminding myself not to yell out to her. I needed to save my energy.

I arched my arms over my head, swimming the best I could against the surf. Inching toward her floating body with each stroke, swimming against the lapping water. I drew closer to the icy shape of her body, and I could see that she was alive.

She lay still in the water, staring upwards. Eyes open. Her hair resting on the surface of the water around her head, splayed out like a sunburst. She rose and fell with each wave. Her steaming breath curled upwards into little wisps that hovered above her lips.

She looked serene.

"Cynthia," I yelled to her, realizing that I was clutching my teeth together. I couldn't feel my face.

I grasped her tiny body with one arm, using my other arm to swim. I drug her body toward the shore, not making much progress against the current. I felt like a one-armed man trying to do the breast stroke.

"Hang on, Cynthia." I tried to shout through a locked jaw. The muscles in my face were seizing, and I my vision growing darker.

"Hang on." I whispered.

My body was numb, almost paralyzed. I could no longer feel my feet, or my legs. I swung my arm over my head, swimming forward with all my might. The stinging sensation was overtaking my torso.

I slowed down, but not on purpose.

A wave crashed over my head.

I swallowed a mouthful of saltwater and then coughed.

I could see my Daddy on the shore, holding an enormous red wooly blanket out in front of him. He flapped it like a flag, back and forth.

"Come on Jimmy!" he called, waving the blanket.

I flashed a weak smile.

He looked like a bull fighter.

58.

I had almost forgotten about the pot of rice on the stove. I ran over to it, hoping that it wasn't already burned. I stirred it and then turned the flame off. I emptied the rice into the strainer and then rinsed the rice underneath the faucet.

"Dinner's almost ready, Daddy," I called, watching the clock above the sink.

I removed the bird from the oven and tossed a handful of flour into the roasting pan, stirring the pure white lumps with a wooden spoon. The flour melded with the dark black chicken drippings, finally converting into a rich brown paste that would become gravy. Loretta's method for making gravy was a simple recipe that was impossible to forget.

Daddy came walking in the kitchen, wearing a thin white undershirt and holding a rolled up newspaper in his hand.

"What time is this girl coming over again?" He was grinning.

"You remember what time." I wiped a smudge of flour off my cheek. "Now go change your shirt, Daddy, she's on her way as we speak."

"What's wrong with this shirt?" He looked down.

"Daddy, go."

He laughed to himself as he left the kitchen.

All three of us sat around our wooden table feeling each other out, being too polite with one another. Daddy looked at the food on the table. The roasted bird, the gravy, rice, butter beans, sliced tomatoes, and my first attempted pound cake, were all positioned on the table cloth as neat as I could arrange them.

Daddy whistled.

"What a spread," Daddy said, looking at Delpha. "Honey, you must be someone awfully special for Jimmy to go to all this trouble."

She blushed, and so did I.

I sliced into the roasted chicken with the carving knife.

"He's good at cutting up a bird," Daddy said.

When Loretta left Daddy, he became a bachelor. And I felt sorry for him. His world became quiet and lonely, it was a life that neither of us would have chosen for each other.

"Dear, God," Daddy said with hands folded. "Thank you for this supper, and for the company around the table. Amen."

"My stars," Delpha said. "It looks delicious."

When the meal was over, I lifted the glass dome off of the pound cake that was seated on Momma's crystal pedestal.

I smiled at the cake. It reminded me of Momma.

I sliced into the cake, and served everyone a slice.

"What, no ice cream?" Daddy said.

Delpha laughed.

Daddy could turn on his folksy charm as easy as flipping a switch, making himself the most amiable man that ever lived. It was part of his job as a public servant, a skill he'd developed, but also a talent that came natural. He could banish any trace of awkwardness with the wink of an eye. That night, there was not a drop of awkwardness in the entire county, Daddy made sure of it.

The three of us sat around the table laughing, sharing stories and learning about each other. It was a ceremony, a formal introduction to the rest of our lives together, the beginning of our collective story. I looked at the empty chair on the other side of the table and closed my eyes. Even though there were only three of us reclining around the table, it felt like there were four.

59.

The fire in my den crackled and popped. Its fork-shaped flames licked the top of the fireplace in a hypnotizing way, turning the bricks black. Staring at the flames, Cynthia and I both inhaled the aroma that filled the den, a piney fragrance. She looked into the fire with a reddened face, and heavy eyes.

Daddy told me that I had passed out on the beach, with Cynthia Alison in my arms, after swimming to shore. He radioed Billy with my handheld, telling him our location. Billy rushed down to the beach in his truck and carted Cynthia and me to my house, which was just down the road a mile. Daddy's distress call that saved my life, rescuing us. I was lucky that Daddy had insisted on coming along with me on my search for Cynthia Alison. Otherwise, I'd be a popsicle, dead, lying on the beach.

I sat on the stone fireplace wrapped in thick blankets, sipping piping hot coffee. My mind was hard at work, lost in an icy haze. I was scrambling to recall my bumbling rescue, from only a few hours earlier. My memories had gone hazy.

I touched my face, it was cold to the touch, and the skin burned. The muscles in my jaw were sore from gritting my teeth while swimming. It was an early symptom of hypothermia, my body's last ditch effort at survival. I knew that because hypothermia was the most common emergency call in our neck of the woods.

Cynthia Alison sat next to me, draped in a wool blanket. The way it wrapped around her head made her look like a saint.

"Your feet are purple," she said, clutching her blanket tight beneath her chin. "Dark purple."

"So is your nose," I said.

Delpha came walking out into the den with a steaming mug of tea; it smelled like oranges and some kind of Christmas spice. There was no telling what flavor it was. Her mammoth collection of tea took up an entire kitchen cabinet. Delpha was a tea addict. It was an addiction I could not quite understand.

"Thank you, Miss Delpha," Cynthia said, taking the mug from Delpha's hands.

I saw Delpha smile at Cynthia, and Cynthia returned the favor. I had not ever seen Cynthia Alison's full kindling smile.

"So I guess you're mad at me, Sheriff?" Cynthia asked.

"No," I said sipping my coffee. I searched for a sentence, but nothing was coming to me.

She studied the blazing fireplace before her, entranced by the yellow light that filled our living room.

She sighed.

"I'm sad about the whole thing." I sat my mug down. "I'm sad at what happened to your mother, and I'm sad at the way it all turned out for you kids. But mostly, I'm sad that you tried to kill yourself."

Cynthia shrugged.

"What's the point of living?" she said. "My mother's life is ruined by what Brian did to her. And now, after what I've done, after what Gabe and Jon Jon have done, all of our lives are going to be ruined forever."

She turned her head back to the fire's glow and let it swallow her cold tarnished face. "Ruined."

Cynthia sipped her tea. Her frostbit face was unsuccessful at covering up her elegance. She sat with her legs crossed, and her back straight. She looked at me with her frostbitten face, and she gathered her eyebrows together.

"I should feel ashamed for the horrid thing that I've done," she said. "But I don't, and I probably never will."

I assumed my father's persona and let myself get as quiet as I could. I observed her and let my ears get big.

"Sheriff, when Momma told me what Brian had done to her, how he had raped her, I wanted to kill him." She narrowed her eyes. "I wanted him to die for what he did. He deserved to die."

She held one hand out toward the warmth of the fire.

"So, I went to a party, down by the creek. You know, at night, where everyone sits around a big campfire and gets drunk. See, I knew Brian would be there. He always hung out at those high school parties, trying to pick up senior girls." She shook her head. "It was downright weird, the way he came to those bonfires; he was the only real adult there. He was a lot older than us.

"I knew he liked me. Well, I mean, I knew he wanted me," she said. "So that night, I waited until he got good and drunk by the campfire, then I lured him out to my car. It was easy; he would've followed me anywhere at that point."

I set my coffee down and noticed how soft her young face was in the firelight. She was a child, hardly old enough to drive a vehicle by herself.

"I had it all worked out beforehand." She closed her eyes. "I had crushed up a whole bottle of Momma's sleeping pills, mixed them with rum and Gatorade, and sweetened it with a lot of sugar."

She looked at me.

I was quiet.

"When I got Brian into my car, it wasn't very hard to convince a drunk like him to drink my Gatorade. He drank it, almost all of it."

I nodded.

"After he drank it, I just waited for a while, letting him kiss me all over." She shivered her shoulders. "Finally, I could tell he was getting really sleepy, so I looked at him, and I just hauled off and slapped him in his face. I hated him so much. I told him to rot in hell for what he did to my mother. It didn't do nothing to him, he probably couldn't feel anything, he just leaned back and laughed, like he was proud of what he did."

Cynthia set her mug down and looked into the fire.

"Well, then I told him that I'd poisoned him, and I told him how I did it, and how he was going to die. I wanted him to think about it as it killed him," she said. "Brian looked at the Gatorade bottle, and smelled it. Then he totally freaked out, started screaming at me, like some kind of monster."

Cynthia lifted up her chin, showing me the little bruises on her neck.

"He did this when he lunged at me. I tried to get out of the car, but he grabbed me by the neck before I could open the driver's door. I screamed while he choked me, fighting against him with all my strength to get him off. It didn't work. He started tearing at my clothes. I thought that he was going to rape me right there."

Tears dropped from her youthful eyes, but she refused to give in to the flood of emotion. She sniffed her nose and dabbed her eyes.

"It got easier to fight against him because he kept getting weaker and weaker from the pills. His arms were flopping around." She wiped her face with her hand. "Eventually, he quit trying to fight me, and started trying to get out of the car. He was having a hard time even moving though. He just started moaning in a low voice, saying, 'You bitch, you little bitch.' And finally, he just passed out in the seat next to me like a dead man."

She paused, then looked at me.

I looked into my mug of coffee.

"I could not believe what I'd done. What's more, I couldn't believe that I'd actually had the courage to go through with it. It was like some terrible nightmare. I looked at his dead body. There Brian Holbrook was in the seat next to me, dead. I took his pulse, and saw that he wasn't dead yet."

She shook her head.

"I didn't know what else to do, so I just drove home. Brian just laid there in the passenger seat next to me, drooling with his head against the window."

"When I parked the car in the driveway, that's when it hit me, I just broke down crying," she said wiping the tears off of her frostbitten cheeks. "I was in total shock. I couldn't even move from the driver's seat. I just sat there and cried in my car, for a long time, until Gabe and Jon Jon got home and found me."

Cynthia ducked her head down.

"I didn't know who else to ask for help. So I asked them to help me get rid of Brian somehow."

Cynthia leaned her back against the warm stone wall next to the fireplace counting the cracks on our living room ceiling. She didn't want to be in my living room, in our town, or in her body. Her life was a terrible costume that she'd been forced to wear.

"See?" she said. "I'm a murderer."

60.

It was a blue truck, slate blue to be exact. It was shiny and brand new.

"Whatcha think?" Daddy asked Delpha and me, looking at the vehicle.

I shrugged. "It's fine, I guess."

The truck didn't match my idea of who Daddy was; it was all wrong. His white truck with the yellow star had become a part of his persona. The old dirty, gravel dinged truck was my father.

"It's lovely," Delpha said.

"Well," I stammered. "It looks like a sturdy truck."

It was all I could think to say. The new truck was horrible, too modern, not dusty enough, no dents.

"Yes, I thought so, too." He patted the vehicle on the hood as if it were a prize-winning cow. "I like the color the best. Slate blue they call it."

Delpha was reclined, swinging on the porch swing of our house, rocking back and forth with her leg dangling. She'd been in the yard all day with me, helping me to haul away a dead tree that had fallen down out back, and her clothes were dirty. She sipped iced tea, watching Daddy try to convince me.

"It's fast," Daddy said it to me as if I cared anything about speed.

"Well, that's nice." I smiled.

"A lot nicer than that old white truck, you know?"

I thought about all the collected time that I'd spent in his old white truck as a child. Hours that added up into days, days that added up into years. It wasn't just the truck that had been lost, it was the years, the whole era. Gone. I was older, and so was he.

"I guess that now you can chase down speeders," I said.

"Exactly," he said nodding, smiling. "Now I can chase down speeders."

"Can you take us for a ride?" Delpha said with a glass of rattling iced sweet tea in her hands.

"Abso-damn-lutely." He nodded.

She knew how to make the old man happy.

Delpha and I piled into the cab of the new truck, I sat in the passenger seat, noticing how different the new truck smelled compared to his old one. It lacked the musty smell that I'd grown up with. It was a smell I came to expect whenever I rode in the old vehicle. The new truck smelled sterile, like fresh leather. I leaned my head back against the window, and Delpha squeezed my hand. I thought about how different our lives were now. Our lives didn't resemble the old lives that we had before Momma fell, our lives were brand new, sterile, like the God-awful new truck.

"No, no Jimmy, don't sit there," Daddy said to me, looking through the window of the driver's door, tossing the jingling keys in my lap.

"This ain't my truck boy," he said. "It's yours."

61.

"Holy Christ," Billy said shaking his head, trying to take it all in. "I would've never guessed that Cynthia Alison was capable of murder, not in a million years."

It was dead silent in my office. Daddy, Hooty, and Billy sat on the opposite side of my desk, just staring at their laps as I recounted the tale of Brian Holbrook. None of us in the room could wrap our heads around the terrible events that had occurred within the Alison family.

Even though I didn't want to think about it, I knew we were all mulling over the same idea. It was my fault. After all, I was charged with protecting the people in our town, more importantly, with protecting their children. I'd failed at both.

"That poor, poor girl," Daddy said, rubbing his white hair. "What's her name again?"

I nodded. "Cynthia."

"Cynthia Alison," Daddy said in a slow voice. "Her daddy was nothing but trouble for this town. Jeezus, seems like a hundred years ago."

"What're you gonna do, Jimmy?" Billy asked.

Hooty and Billy looked at me. Hooty's eyelids pinched together, his mouth was drawn tight.

"What a mess," Daddy rose and walked to the window. "It's almost as if the Alison's are cursed."

I thrusted my hands into my pockets.

Daddy looked out the window into the November sky. The grayish clouds outdoors hung low to the ground, swooping up and down, in and out, like upside-down rolling hills. It was one of those days that threatened rain, but it didn't have the gumption to follow through.

"Hooty, do you remember Johnny Biltmore?" Daddy said in a soft dry voice.

Hooty looked at Daddy then back at me, readjusting himself in his chair.

"Of course you do." Daddy breathed on the window, fogging it up with his breath, then drew a smiley face on the pane with his finger. "Who could forget him? Johnny Biltmore was a hateful man. Downright evil," Daddy said. "Biltmore scalded his three-year-old daughter with a pot of boiling water. And you know, I think it was the absolute worst thing I ever saw. Worse than anything I ever saw over in Europe. You remember that night, Hooty?"

Hooty said nothing.

"She was a beautiful little girl, too. Curly blonde hair, freckles." Daddy tapped on the window. "Johnny got so mean drunk one night that he poured a whole pot of boiling water on the little girl. Poured it over her shoulders and neck, down the little girl's front and backside."

Daddy rubbed his chin.

"The little girl's skin looked like a roasted duck by the time we got to her. Red, pink, and bubbly, bleeding all over," Daddy said. "She was twisted on the floor, wrenching in pain, screaming like a wounded animal. I won't never forget that scream, it was so unusual." Daddy sighed. "So very unusual."

Hooty shook his head.

"So, Johnny Biltmore was sitting in the corner when we got there, smoking, paying no attention to his daughter. He'd sobered up a bit by that time. He wasn't even concerned about the little girl. He just sat there, watching her wallow on the floor like a dog."

Hooty looked at Daddy through the corner of his eye, without turning his head.

"Well, I lifted Johnny up by the shirt collar, and threw him down the steps of his own porch. My whole world turned to red when I saw Johnny looking at me with that face. I couldn't think clearly. I didn't really know what I was doing – but I knew, by God, I was doing right."

Hooty looked at me and nodded.

"I told that bastard to run. To run as fast as he damn well could. To get as far away from there as his puny legs would carry him." Daddy paused. "And he did just that. Johnny ran down that empty dirt road like a jackrabbit."

Daddy looked at me.

"And then I shot him," Daddy said. "Dead."

The room had dimmed to complete silence.

I thought that I had seen every facet of Daddy's personality, the good, and the ugly alike, but I was wrong. The man standing by the window was a creature unfamiliar to me.

A vigilante.

"The way I sees it," Daddy said. "Sometimes evil infects a man like a disease. The disease eats him up inside, consuming his organs, weaving its way into his bones. Then it crawls up to his head and gets all in his mind. Before you know it, the man starts to froth at the mouth like a rabid dog, raising the hair on his neck, baring his teeth. You look into his eyes, and you can tell he ain't even in his body no more, just the disease."

I clasped my hands together and looked down at my desk. I tried to visualize my Daddy as a younger man. I remembered his brown hair, his wide brimmed hat, his gun.

"Dammit, Lawrence is right." Hooty stood up. "It's a simple fact of living. Everyone knows there's only one way to handle a rabid dog."

62.

Lily White was the name of the paint color that we picked out. It was a shade of white somewhere between school-paper-white, and the light color of vanilla ice cream. It was the closest match to the color of our old house that the hardware store had in stock.

There were four of us in the painting crew that day. Tasks were divided equal among us. While Daddy and I stood high upon ladders, painting with thick bristle brushes, Delpha and Hooty scraped using stiff wire brushes. Everyone had their own brush to bear. Delpha and Hooty were covered in white flecks of dried paint. It looked like they were covered in snow.

"Miss Dell is a better worker than I am," Hooty said before taking a bite of his tomato sandwich. "A lot faster than old Paw-Paw Hooty."

Daddy looked at the house, he was covered in globs of paint, streaks of Lily White covered his clothes like zebra stripes.

"You better pick up the pace, Paw Paw Hooty," Delpha said. "Or I'm gonna fire you from the painting crew."

"Well, well," Hooty said. "Step aside, Sheriff, there's a new sheriff in town. And she's a sight prettier than the last one, I must admit."

Daddy chuckled and took a swig of his beer. "Well, Dell, you can have the job if you want it." Daddy set his beer down. "I've decided I'm not running for Sheriff this term."

The murmur of our laughter faded.

Hooty stared at Daddy.

"You joking, Lawrence?" Hooty asked.

"Afraid not."

Hooty nodded once.

Daddy and Hooty had run the roads together since the earth cooled, they were as tight of friends as any in our county.

Hooty blinked.

"Well, I can understand that." Hooty picked up his beer. "God knows I can understand that old boy. It's a lot of damned pressure to do your job."

Hooty took a pull from his beer and swallowed the lump in his throat.

"Who could even replace you?" Delpha said.

"Could be Sawyer, or even Michael Lancaster," Daddy said. "Neither of them would run against me, they'd only run if they had my blessing. They're good fellas."

"Michael Lancaster?" I said. "As Sheriff?"

"My daddy used to go hunting with Mister Lancaster," Delpha said.

Hooty stood wiping his face with his forearm. He brushed the paint flakes from his clothes. I watched him walked away from our little lunch group to the back of the house.

Daddy looked at the house.

I thought about the people who Daddy had hurt in his life, by just being who he was. Me. Loretta. Hooty was another name on the list.

63.

The drive to Cedar Port was pretty one. Our old bridge arcs across the bay like a cement rainbow on stilts. While driving the middle portion of the bridge, along the apex of the curve, you can look out your car windows and see nothing but a mesa of blue water for miles. It's spectacular, like a navy blue desert.

The medical examiner lied to me. She said that it would take four to six weeks to send in a toxicology report. It only took three. The plastic white envelope sat next to me in the passenger seat of my truck as I drove across the bridge into Cedar Port. Inside the white envelope were documents outlining Brian Holbrook's demise. The front page of the report read that Brian had died from an overdose of Triazolam, a potent sleeping medication. The concentration of the drug in Brian's blood was thirty times the prescribed amount.

He didn't have a chance.

I pulled up to the curb of the little brick house, it had seen better days. It was a decrepit structure covered in the green mold stains from Floridian humidity. Clumps of damp pine straw covered the roof like red fur, dropped there by the tall long leafs that surrounded the house. The home was, by all means, a poster-house for the impoverished.

Gabe's aluminum Jon Boat was parked next to the old garage, encased in the tall weeds that grew around it, his old yellow truck was parked crooked in the driveway.

I walked the path to their front door, my boots clomping on the cold dirt. I rapped on their weathered front door. After knocking, I took a few steps back.

The entire Alison family met me at the front door. They gathered together, shoulder to shoulder on the stoop. Glenda, Gabe, Jon Jon, and

Cynthia Alison each looked at me with intense eyes, not knowing which one of them I was coming for.

I looked upward at the pines. The trees congregated around us, looking down on us, like a jury of ancient Indians. I hitched my hands in my pockets and noticed a tuft of vapor escaping my mouth.

"How's everyone enjoying this November weather today?" I asked.

Glenda folded her arms across her chest.

"Just get it over with, Sheriff," Gabe said, wringing his hands together. "We all know why you're here."

I nodded. "Fair enough."

Cynthia looked at me with a stiff face.

I fumbled the white envelope from my coat and then cleared my throat.

"Upon a thorough forensic examination of the deceased, the coroner has determined a cause of death for Brian Holbrook."

I looked up from the document in my hands.

"I, uh, thought that it might be best if I delivered the news in person."

"Get on with it," Cynthia said.

I cleared my throat again.

"Well, it was determined, by the county's medical examiner, that the deceased, Brian Holbrook, expired from an overdose of Triazolam."

The family's faces were tense. The Alisons were waiting for me to speak in plain English.

I tucked the envelope back into my jacket.

"What I mean to say is," I said. "The county has ruled Brian's death as a suicide."

64.

"This is absurd," Daddy said. "Who ever heard of an election party? Don't get me wrong, I'm glad Michael won, but hell, no one even ran against him."

It was a rare thing to see Daddy's ego come out to play.

"If you ask me…." Daddy hooked his arm around Delpha's. "Sawyer should've run, he's older, would've been wiser."

Delpha walked next to Daddy up the little stone walkway in the dark while I stayed close behind.

"It's a sweet gesture for you to come to the party, Lawrence," she said putting her arm around Daddy's.

Standing in front of the reception hall doors, in the rear of the church, was Mister Lancaster, our soon-to-be lawman. It was hard to envision him as the new Sheriff, the look on his face that seemed so wide eyed and innocent compared to Daddy's. I didn't quite know how to feel about him.

It was a strange feeling for me to imagine a young man like him taking over a role that Daddy created. Lancaster drove a nicer truck than Daddy, and dressed sharper. I'd never known sheriff's to indulge in such things.

"Sheriff," Michael said, greeting Daddy. "Thanks for coming tonight."

Daddy shook the younger man's hand and smiled. The lines on Daddy's face made shadows on his cheeks.

"Aw, I wouldn't've missed it for the world, Michael." Daddy pumped the man's hand. "Congratulations, son."

I wrinkled my face at my Daddy's comment. Daddy did not

congratulate people.

Michael turned and opened the double doors to the fellowship hall with a grand sweep of his arm. The doors flung open, and the room erupted with a deafening applause, like a colossal waterfall of clapping hands.

Daddy stood still, facing the room of two hundred folks, all dressed in their Sunday best. They stood, smiling, applauding beneath a large hand painted sign strung up from the rafters. It read: Goodbye Sheriff.

"What in the hell?" Daddy said.

All Daddy could do was blink.

Hooty came prancing up to Daddy, clapping his hands as fast as a hummingbird flutters its wings, with a bottle of beer tucked underneath his arm.

He leaned into Daddy's ear, "I tried to send them all home, but I guess these damn fools couldn't wait until you were dead to speak highly of you."

65.

I don't listen to the radio in my truck. It's not that I don't like music, I like it well enough. But for me, it's something about the silence that I like better. The quiet feels more sacred, more honest – whatever that means. Music is nice, but it muddies up the clean air sometimes.

I looked at the radio and decided to turn it on.

I adjusted the little knob to the left, and then to the right. The radio hissed and scratched like an angry kitten. There was a lot of loud music out there that I didn't recognize; I'd been away from the popular music too long, I suppose. I snapped the radio off. The world and its music seemed to have gone on without me. Even though they were writing new songs, using new instruments, they were more or less singing about the same things.

Through my windshield, I spotted a vacant yellow truck parked on the side of the road with an empty boat trailer attached.

I knew that truck.

I clomped out of the driver's seat and onto the soft ground, pulling my coat collar up. There was a stiffness in the air that nipped at the corners of my mouth, cracking my lips. It was nasty weather.

I walked down onto the shore, where the bay meets the sand, and I saw them out on the water, Gabe and Jon Jon. They didn't look very happy, but they didn't look sad either. I hoped that one day they'd make peace with what had happened to them, though I'm not quite sure how something like that's even done. I don't know how anyone finds peace or happiness in this world, I'm not sure it even exists in its pure form. I think I've always liked easiness better than happiness anyhow. I think an easy life is better than a happy one.

I looked down at the water. I could see through it, like a pane of glass. The shells and pebbles underneath the water looked like a collage of colors. If you stare at the colors long enough, they mix, and blend into a gray.

I listened to the gentle water scoop the shore with a lapping sound. The waves broke on the shore like a melody, like a song. Truth be told, I don't much care for songs; they've never done that much for me, but the sound of the bay is the prettiest song I've ever heard.

I was glad to see the boys out on the water though they never saw me standing there. It cheered me to see them doing what simple people like me do. Fishing the bay at either sun up, or at sundown, but never in between.

ABOUT THE AUTHOR

Sean Dietrich is a columnist, humorist, and novelist, known for his commentary on life in the American South. His columns have appeared in *South Magazine,* the *Bitter Southerner, Thom Magazine, Tallahassee Democrat,* and he has authored six books and three novels.

An avid sailor and fisherman, when he's not writing, he spends much of his time aboard his sailboat *(The S.S. Squirrel),* along with his coonhound, Ellie Mae.